# Murder at the Clocktower

*A Golden Restoration Mystery*

## Diana Orgain

Lemonade Press, LLC

# Contents

1. Chapter One — 1
2. Chapter Two — 7
3. Chapter Three — 12
4. Chapter Four — 17
5. Chapter Five — 21
6. Chapter Six — 24
7. Chapter Seven — 28
8. Chapter Eight — 33
9. Chapter Nine — 37
10. Chapter Ten — 41
11. Chapter Eleven — 46
12. Chapter Twelve — 50
13. Chapter Thirteen — 55
14. Chapter Fourteen — 60
15. Chapter Fifteen — 65
16. Chapter Sixteen — 71
17. Chapter Seventeen — 75
18. Chapter Eighteen — 79
19. Chapter Nineteen — 84
20. Chapter Twenty — 88

| | |
|---|---|
| Also by Diana Orgain | 94 |
| Copyright | 96 |

# Chapter One

Thanks to the rising price of gold, my hometown of Golden, California was in the midst of an unprecedented economic boost. That was one of the reasons I was returning home for the first time in over five years.

Nerves fluttering through my belly as I parked my car, hiding under a sunhat and glasses. My hometown hosted many faces I didn't care to revisit, as well as a hoard of memories I didn't want to relive.

But sometimes, that's what being an adult is all about, facing traumas and ghosts, trying to better oneself despite them. At least, that's what my therapist said. And goodness knows, I'd done my best to avoid both her advice and my trauma by practicing Balasana on the beach in Bali.

For the time being, only one person knew that I was back: my childhood best friend, Tori Kemp.

Despite my anxiety, I walked into the small café on the outskirts of Golden. With chipped paint and discolored tiles, the café was in desperate need of updating, but that was hardly surprising. The café had been here for over fifty years. It'd been my favorite place to visit with Steven.

Steven.

My throat tightened at the thought of him, and I pushed down the painful emotions bubbling in my chest. Across the open space, I spotted Tori in a corner booth. We had ruled the schoolyard together and seeing her now warmed my heart.

She leapt out the booth and launched herself at me, giggling as she threw her arms around my neck. I realized that, even though Tori and I were both in our late thirties, she still had a youthfulness about her that I'd long abandoned.

Tori is everything I'm not.

She was a small-town girl with roots as deep as an ancient oak. And I'm fairly certain she'd never once ventured outside of the county limits for any extended period of time. On the other hand, I had spent the first year of my five-year absence in Bali, learning to meditate and making worldwide connections before relocating to Los Angeles for my career in architecture.

While I rose the ranks of the design world, Tori rose the ranks of Golden, becoming an influential leader in our hometown. It was these two paths that now brought us together. I had intentionally chosen this location, knowing I was less likely to bump into someone I knew, the further away from town we were. Once seated, I adjusted my sunglasses and large hat, and Tori smirked in my direction.

"You know," she said, glancing over the top of her menu. "The disguise is a bit much."

I laughed. "I'm not wearing a disguise, Tori."

"It certainly looks that way," Tori said. "Take off the hat and sunglasses, would you?"

I glanced around the café before removing them, placing them next to me in the booth. "This is weird for me, being back," I admitted.

"I know," she said. "Honestly, when I called you with the job offer, I really didn't think you'd take it. Don't get me wrong; I'm glad you did. I've missed you."

"I'm sorry I've been so out of touch lately," I said. "Things have been pretty crazy in LA."

"So you've told me." She leaned forward on the table, sighing melodramatically. "If work has been so busy… I'm curious why you're sitting across from me now. You said you never wanted to come back to Golden. So, why take me up on my offer?"

"Renovating something unique like Golden's historical clocktower will color up my resume. Sure, work has been decent in LA, but it's all boring cookie cutter industrial parks and office buildings. If I want to get serious in my career, I need a change, something other than boxy buildings in my portfolio. And I can do it well. I like the artsy challenge that comes with this job."

The café's server scurried over to take our order.

I ordered a ham and cheese panini with caramelized onions, a side salad, and coffee.

Tori said, "Same, but with fries not salad." She flashed me a wicked smile and shrugged. "You know me."

The coffees arrived so quickly Tori was hardly able to show me pictures of her son, Nolan. He'd finished kindergarten now; he had been just a baby the last time I'd been in town.

"He's beautiful," I told her as she put down her phone and poured a gob-smacking amount of sugar into her black coffee. I grinned. "You haven't changed. I'm glad to know my favorite Golden girl is still Golden as ever."

"So are you, Hope," Tori said. "I'll show you more Nolan pictures later. Right now, I'm dying to talk business with you."

I nodded. "I'm all business these days."

Tori sipped her coffee, making a weak attempt to hide her sad smile. "The committee's meeting in the next few days, and they'd like to hear your pitch not only for the clocktower but for the museum and for the

Golden Miner statue as well. The clocktower being the most pressing, of course."

"Let me guess, the old legend still ringing true?" I asked, and Tori nodded.

The town of Golden had been riddled with superstitious nuts, going back all the way to our Gold Rush mining roots. Legend said the town would only be prosperous so long as the clocktower was functioning. A freshly redone clocktower was bound to bring some of that Golden, California luck, especially with the influx of tourists the place was now experiencing.

"All right, so they want the clocktower done first, and I'm guessing they want it done quickly so it's not down for long. And done well." I grinned, then sipped my coffee.

"Fast and perfect," Tori said. "Which is why I recommended you. My spot on the committee got you a place in the lineup, but it's not going to guarantee they hire you."

"Of course," I agreed.

"You need to really wow them with your proposal," Tori said. "It needs to be beautiful, have a detailed plan on how you're going to get it done, and it needs to be within budget."

I smiled. "This isn't my first rodeo, Tori. My first clocktower renovation maybe, but not my first time bidding on a job."

She chuckled. "I know. Sorry. I just would love for you to land this one."

I nodded, scribbling down a few ideas in my notebook. "Clocktower done first..." I said my voice catching.

I swallowed the lump in my throat, and Tori gave me a sympathetic look.

I'd shared my first kiss with my husband, Steven, at that clocktower. A lot of locals had similar nostalgic feelings. There was something romantic about the antique tower, and that was something I planned on keeping when I worked on the redesign. I needed to preserve that classical yet whimsical quality. I suspected the committee felt similarly.

The lump in my throat grew to a knot in my stomach as I thought about Steven. He was the reason I had left Golden. After ten years of a happy marriage, I lost him to a tragic kayaking accident.

Now, everything in Golden reminded me of him.

The clocktower especially.

"Are you going to be able to do this, Hope?" Tori asked. "You don't have to do it for me, you know? I called you because I know you understand what the clocktower represents for the town, but you don't have to do it for my sake."

I flashed her an entirely unconvincing smile. "I told you. My resume needs the boost," I said. "And, once it's all done, I'll be back in LA where I belong. Small towns... not really my thing anymore. I prefer big cities. Places like this make me feel claustrophobic."

Tori nodded as though she understood.

But how can she?

Tori loved Golden. And Golden loved Tori. Every local knew her name and she relished the familiarity and comfort. She loved being a big fish in a small-town.

But me… in Golden again…

"Order up, Tori!" the server said playfully as she placed our paninis in front of us. "Can I get you ladies anything else?"

"I think we're good," Tori said. "You, Hope?"

"I'm fine, thank you," I said, and the server trotted off.

"So, when are you going to stop hiding in a motel outside town?" Tori asked. "There's plenty of little inns and rental homes closer to where you'll be working, if you get the job."

"I know," I said, taking a bite of my ham and cheese panini. "Didn't want to jump on a rental right out of the gate, though. You said I had some competition, right?"

Tori rolled her eyes. "If you can call it that. Some big conglomerate called Revival."

I nearly choked on my food. I gulped down some coffee to clear my throat before speaking. "I'm up against Revival Architecture?"

"Is that bad?"

"Tori!" I exclaimed. "They're the name for small town renovations in the west. For starters, there's no way I could ever match their prices."

"Their ideas suck," Tori said. "They're too… what was the phrase you used? Cookie cutter. They want to get in, get paid, and get out. You're a Golden girl—"

"A girl from Golden," I corrected, and we laughed.

"My point is, you know what this town needs better than these guys in suits. You know what the clocktower means to us, and you know how to keep that Golden charm. These people don't know anything about Golden and our history. They're going to come in with some ridiculous idea, I'm sure of it."

"I don't know—"

Tori waved her hand about, dismissing me. "Please. You are our small-town Hope."

Doubt, disguised as a headache, wedged itself into my temples. "How on earth did Revival Architecture even come into play? They don't have an office up this way, do they?"

Tori fidgeted with her napkin and looked out the window.

"Did they open up a new office?" I asked.

Tori glanced back from the window, then shoved a handful of fries into her mouth. If I didn't know her, I might have been fooled, but she looked to me like she was avoiding the question.

I stared her down, silently waiting for a response. At last, Tori sighed. "The president of the renovation committee wants them. Bad. And he's a hard man to impress."

"Really?" I questioned. "Who is he? Anyone I know?"

"Maybe..."

"Tori," I said sternly. "What aren't you telling me?"

Tori again hesitated, but at last she muttered, "Dustin Peterson."

The name pummeled me in the chest. "Dustin?" I asked. "My high school fling? Steven's best friend? He's the one I'm going to be pitching this idea to?"

"He is one of several you'll be pitching to, and he has no more sway than me," Tori assured me.

I thought back to high school graduation when Dustin and I had broken things off. That was a lifetime ago, but it had hit Dustin hard. He'd been angry and bitter, and I'd honestly only made it worse by getting involved with his best friend, Steven. Their relationship was awkward for a while, but Dustin and Steven reconciled.

Not that that meant Dustin had forgiven me.

I rubbed my temples. "Tori, how could you not tell me Dustin is on the committee? That he's the president of the committee! That he's already looking at another architectural firm?"

Her eyes grew wide, and she stared at me. "You know why!"

I chuckled despite myself. "Because I wouldn't come to Golden?"

Tori slammed her hand down on the table. "Exactly! And I know you can win the committee over even if Dustin is dead set against you doing it."

"But I'm going to be working with him, right?" I asked. "You should have told me Dustin was going to be part of this."

"You two were high school sweethearts," Tori said. "That was so long ago. Are you seriously telling me you're thinking about copping out because of Dustin?"

I crossed my arms and leaned back into the booth. "No, I'm not. Obviously, I'm still going to submit the proposal. I just hate that it means seeing Dustin. I was hoping to run into as few people I know as possible."

"If you get the job, you're going to be here for a while, Hope," Tori said. "It's not just the clocktower, remember? That alone will take several months, but the museum and the statue of the Golden Miner are going to add to that exponentially. You're going to bump into people you know if you're going to be staying in town that long."

I sighed. "I know," I said, fingering my sandwich and finally pushing it aside. "I figured I'd probably run into him eventually. Golden's not exactly a huge city. I just didn't think I'd be dealing with Dustin so soon."

"A place where everyone knows your name," Tori said. "Can't believe you'd hate that."

"Can't believe you'd love it," I grumbled.

Tori laughed, and I begrudgingly uncrossed my arms. "It is good to see you. I've missed you. Occasional video chats and a Christmas card is really not the same as sitting down for lunch, is it?"

"No, it really isn't," Tori said. "Welcome home, Hope."

"Don't say that," I countered. "LA is my home now."

"If you say so," Tori said, taking another bite of her panini. "So, lay it on me. What do you have so far?"

I dug into my leather satchel and retrieved a file I'd been working on since Tori's email last weekend. I spread it across the table. Tori gasped, then clamped a hand over her mouth.

I eyed her, a smile playing on my lips. "Do you like the concept?"

Tori jammed a finger onto my pages and squealed. "Those suits from Revival can't compare to this," she said. "You got this!"

"We'll see," I said skeptically. "Revival really knows what they're doing. I'm not going to lie, I'm worried about that one. Almost as worried as presenting this to Dustin."

"I'll be there," Tori said. "I'm obviously on the committee too. And so are a lot of other friendly faces from your past, hon. And, when you show them this, they're going to be blown away. Revival and Dustin will be impressed."

"Thanks, Tori," I said. "Honestly, I really want this to work. Even if that means spending time in Golden. This project will give my resume the jump it needs to get the sort of jobs I'm after."

Tori sipped her coffee and gave me a mischievous grim. "No more boxy office buildings for you. You're back in Golden and going to stay, if I can help it."

I chuckled. "That's what I'm afraid of."

# Chapter Two

I knew this would happen eventually. For the last two days I'd been surviving on eggs and potato chips, in denial of what needed to be done: a grocery run. I'd stuffed my bags with enough food to avoid having to leave the motel until after the committee meeting, but now the meeting had been pushed back a week, and I was down to half a slice of bread and a half-empty jar of mayonnaise.

I was in a rather unfortunate predicament.

I could go to a store outside of town, I thought and whipped out my phone to see where the nearest store was that was outside of Golden.

Anything to avoid going home just yet.

"An extra fifteen minutes just to get off the freeway..." I mumbled.

Looking at the time, I knew that fifteen minutes was a grand underestimation given the traffic outside of town. Golden might have been a small town, but it was surrounded by larger cities with heavy traffic. I was bound to get caught up in an early lunch rush.

"Am I really going to drive thirty minutes to avoid bumping into anyone I know?" I asked aloud, staring at the keys in the little bowl by the door. "Maybe I could just grab lunch at that sandwich shop again..." But I really didn't need to spend frivolously when I wasn't certain I'd land the clocktower renovation job.

The tiny one-bed motel room had been more than enough in the past two weeks, but it was already beginning to feel cramped. Sooner or later, if I managed to get the job, I was going to have to get some sort of rental closer to town.

Maybe I should go to town for groceries, pick up a local paper while I'm there. See if there are any rooms for rent...

"Nah," I said at last, snagging my keys from the bowl and my purse from the bedside table. As I made my way to where I had parked the evening before, I had an obnoxious thought.

Do you really want your first time in town to be the day of the committee meeting? What if you have some sort of panic attack or something?

"Dang you, inner-dialogue," I said. But it was a serious concern I hadn't considered before. There was a reason I hadn't returned to Golden in so long. The very thought of going back into town had me hiding just outside its borders in a motel near the freeway.

I stood at the driver's side of my white Porsche, staring at the dent and bright blue line just below the handle where I was side-swiped not thirty minutes after buying it.

I'd wanted a Porsche since I'd been a teenager. I always thought if I had reached that goal, it would be my "I made it" moment. That moment had me jumping out of the car thirty minutes later, shouting at a woman who had broken down in tears over it. I'd never lost my head like that before, and I felt terrible for reacting the way I had. My "I made it" moment had been soiled, not because of the accident but because of how I responded to it. I'd been harboring so much rage for so long that it finally exploded on some poor woman who hadn't yielded at a roundabout.

So, I left the damage.

It was a reminder to not let myself get dragged too far into the world of money games again. My materialist ways had taken a hit for me, and ironically, the shape of the blue from the other woman's car… it looked like the clocktower.

Perhaps that was really what sent me over the edge?

Truthfully, I hadn't been angry until after I had seen the image of the clocktower staring back at me, forcing me to think about Golden for the first time in a while. The accident had only been a few weeks ago; I had gotten the call from Tori only a few short hours later, asking me about the clocktower. It was as good for a sign as any that it was time for me to visit Golden again.

Even if it was only temporary.

I exhaled, yanked open the car door, and jammed myself in the driver's seat. "Golden," I muttered, putting the car in reverse and pulling out of the motel's parking lot. "Can't believe I'm going to Golden… for groceries, of all things…" I gripped the steering wheel until my knuckles turned white.

The motel was a good distance from Golden's grocery store, and I prayed I'd be lucky enough to avoid anyone from the past.

Five years was a long time to be gone from a small town like Golden.

I checked my reflection in the rear-view mirror.

I had grown my hair out, and before I didn't have highlights. It was more of an LA style now; long, curled, and generally well kept. Not the traditional ponytail and ballcap some of the Golden women were used to.

Maybe if I do see someone I know, they won't recognize me…

Not likely!

I glanced over in my passenger's seat to the sunglasses and sunhat I'd worn the day I'd met Tori. I snagged the sunglasses, putting them on before pulling into the parking lot of the grocery store. It was a small mom-and-pop store that ran a pretty big risk of attracting other locals, so I didn't want to take any chances. Once I was parked, I put the hat on as well and double checked myself in the mirror, pulling it down to shadow more of my face.

"Nothing like the Hope Wilson who left five years ago, I'd say," I muttered to myself, taking a deep breath and climbing out of the car. My phone buzzed. It was Tori. I huffed as I answered it. "You better not be calling me to tell me they postponed the committee meeting again. Or that you made the whole thing up to get me in Golden! Because if you are, I'm going to teepee your house before I speed back to LA."

Tori laughed. "No, nothing like that. And, careful, don't work out my diabolical plans just yet, please."

"Funny."

"I'm just checking to see how you're doing. I know you weren't expecting to have to wait around a whole other week, but Revival wanted more time after they heard we had someone else giving a proposal as well," Tori explained. "Sounds like your name ruffled some feathers when I talked with their rep. Looks like Revival isn't the only architect around here with a reputation."

"Sounds like they don't know what they're doing if they're intimidated by Hope Wilson," I teased. I entered the shop, pulling my hat down another inch just to be on the safe side. "You weren't talking me up to everyone, were you? If this doesn't pan out, I'd rather not get stuck having to meet a bunch of people who want to play catch up."

"You still just hanging out at the motel trying to avoid everyone?" Tori asked, and I cringed.

"If you must know, I have left the motel," I said. "Had to do a grocery run. I'm officially in Golden."

"Oh my goodness," Tori said, laughing. "Please tell me you're not wearing your disguise again."

"Err..." I muttered, grabbing a grocery cart and making my way down the first aisle.

"You're ridiculous!"

"Oh, shut up!" I said. "Right now, I'm debating on whether or not to get groceries for just another week or if I should play it safe and get enough for two..."

"Get enough for two, so it'll last you until after you get the job," Tori said excitedly. "But then again, if that happens—which it will—you'll get a place closer to town, I assume. And you don't want to have to move a bunch of groceries from the motel to wherever you wind up. So... maybe just shoot for a weeks' worth? I'm going to drag you out to eat at least one more time before the committee meeting. We could go rental shopping together tomorrow and grab lunch if you want?"

"I can't even think about that right now." I grabbed a few cans from the shelves, including baked beans. I could make tacos one night. I didn't have much to do at the motel other than work on my presentation and plan out meals, so I resisted the urge to buy too much processed stuff. In the past few days, I'd snacked really badly out of boredom.

"You want the job. The job means staying in Golden for a while, you know?" Tori said. "You can handle that, can't you, Hope?"

"I can handle it," I said, though I didn't feel it. Tori didn't catch my tone.

"If you can handle it, stop wearing a disguise to the store," Tori insisted. "Look, I know this is hard for you, but you can't keep hidden forever."

I exhaled. "Fine. Fine! I'm taking the hat off—jerk!" I laughed, yanking my hat off. "Look, let me finish shopping, and I'll call you later. Maybe we can do brunch tomorrow?"

"Ooh, are you going to wear a Halloween mask to brunch?"

"Hanging up now, Tori," I said. "Talk to you tomorrow." I hung up the phone, stuffing my hat into the cart and removing my sunglasses. She's probably right. I am being overly dramatic.

"Hope?"

My heart leapt as I spun around and came eye to eye with the one person I wanted to avoid more than anyone else: Dustin Peterson. For a split moment, I contemplated how to react. Hide? Pretend not to see him? Lie and act like he was confused and mistaken me for someone else? Smile? Be excited? Were we on handshake or hug terms?

"Hey, Dustin," I said as plainly as I could.

He blinked like he thought he was seeing a ghost.

My breath caught.

Dustin hadn't changed a bit, he had the same rugged features and dazzling eyes.

"What are you doing here?" he asked, taking a few anxious steps closer, like he thought I'd disappear if he came too close. "When did you get back in town?"

"Um," I said, realizing instantly Dustin had no idea why I was there. Hadn't Tori told him who was going to be putting in a proposal at the committee meeting? "I'm not exactly back," I said. "Well, I might be. We'll see, I suppose. I may have a job out this way."

"In Golden?" he asked, looking skeptical. "You disappear for, what's it been, five years? And you come back suddenly for a job? Did life in LA not pan out for you?"

I crossed my arms and smirked. "Last time we spoke I was heading out to Bali. How'd you know I landed in LA? You been spying on me online or something?"

Dustin had never been one to get frazzled from embarrassment, but he took a step back. "Well, I, um…"

I couldn't help myself. I laughed. "I'm just kidding, Dustin."

"People talk," he said. "I'm sure I heard it from Tori. She and I are on the town committee together now. You two are still chummy, right?"

"Of course," I said. "I know I've been gone, but I haven't completely disconnected from Golden."

Dustin was quiet. He switched his grocery basket his right hand to his left and stood up a bit taller, a thought seeming to have occurred to him. "Tori…" he muttered. "You're here for the restoration of the clocktower! You're the other bid, aren't you?"

I took a breath. "Yes, Dustin, that's me."

He cocked his head back. "Work that bad you've got to get your high school friend to try to get you a job back in your hometown? That's just sad."

I put my hands on my hips unable to believe his nerve.

"I know you did not just say that to me," I said. "I'm interested in the job because it's going to look good on my resume. I need to spice it up, so when Tori called me and told me Golden was looking for an architect, I decided to throw my name in the hat."

"Of course you did," he said, sounding gravely disappointed. "You know you're going up against Revival, right? They specialize in revitalizing small towns, hence the name. Do you even have anything like that on your resume? Have you ever done anything other than a few office buildings in LA?"

I laughed at him. "Oh, wow, you really have been creeping on me online, haven't you? You checking out what I've been up to, Dustin?"

"I told you I'm not," he countered. "Well, whatever. Welcome back to Golden, I suppose."

"Why do you have an attitude with me, Dustin?" I asked.

"You know what, I'm getting into it in a grocery store," he said. "You just finish your shopping. I'm sorry I said anything. Should have just pretended I didn't see you."

"Yeah, you probably should have," I said and then took a breath. "Dustin, I'm sorry. I wasn't expecting to run into you."

"I certainly wasn't expecting to see you either," he admitted and then took a calming breath as well. "I'm sorry. You just took me off guard, that's all. I don't mean to be hostile. I'll leave you alone, let you do your shopping. I suppose I'll see you at the committee meeting ."

"Yes," I said. "I'll see you then."

We walked off in opposite directions. I'm going to kill Tori for talking me into taking my hat and glasses off!

# Chapter Three

I sat in my car the morning of the meeting with the restoration committee, my heart pounding. My run-in with Dustin had been bad enough; I couldn't imagine who I'd potentially run into at the town center if I dared to actually step outside of my car. I had driven through town late several times since Tori first told me about the job, looking at the clocktower and picking up blueprints. But coming in the middle of the day was a different story.

"You can do this, you big baby," I said to myself, sitting upright and turning my rearview mirror towards myself. "Your meeting is in two minutes, and you're not even sure what room it's in… so why are you still sitting here like a big dope?"

I took a deep breath, and as I reached for the handle, I spotted Dustin hurrying across the parking lot. He was dressed in a flattering suit, a small briefcase at his side. "Typical Dustin," I muttered. He always overdressed, and the briefcase was just a step too far for the occasion.

Glancing in the direction he was sprinting, I saw a young man in an even more uppity business suit with an even more unnecessarily fancy briefcase. They met and shook hands. There were two other gentlemen standing on either side, and he seemed to be introducing Dustin to the group.

"Must be the reps from Revival," I muttered, realizing they were likely about to be escorted by the president of the committee to the meeting room.

My phone buzzed for the eighth time, and at last I answered it, climbing out of the car in the process. "Don't be mad," I said, hurrying around to the back of the car to grab everything I needed for the presentation.

"I swear, if you dip out and make me look stupid, Hope, I'm going to hunt you down and—"

"I'm here, Tori," I assured her. I locked eyes with Dustin from across the parking lot. Wanting to maintain a sense of professionalism, we waved awkwardly in front of the Revival members. One of their team was evidently a gentleman, because he walked over to me upon realizing I had a load to carry. "I'm coming in. Will see you shortly," I said.

"You must be Hope Wilson," the man said in the most pleasant tone I had ever heard from a fellow Californian. "Please, let me help you."

"Oh, it's fine," I said, but truthfully, I knew my presentation would take two trips, and I was already running late.

"I insist," he said. "I'm Sonny. Sonny Bono, and no, that's not a joke. No relation."

I snickered. "Funny. Nice to meet you, Sonny. I'm sorry. Clearly your parents had quite a sense of humor."

"They really did. My sister is named Cher. And that's no joke either. Try going through high school with you and your twin sister being named after a married duo."

I laughed as Dustin and the other two gentlemen begrudgingly made their way over. "Don't tell me, you told her about your sister," one of the other men said, and Sonny laughed.

"You know I always introduce us both whether she's here or not to explain my silly name," he said. "Plus, it's a great ice breaker."

"Get over yourself, Sonny," the first man said, laughing.

"You must be our competition today," said the other, offering me his hand. "Adam Douglas. This is Bradley Wilks. And I'm assuming you know Dustin?"

"I know Dustin," I said as Sonny put a handful of my materials in Dustin's hands like he was a mule. I bit my lip to keep from smirking.

"Always a pleasure, Hope," Dustin said, hiding his irritation.

It was awkward walking in with Dustin and my rather formidable competition, but at least this meant we were all arriving together, so when we walked in nearly five minutes after the meeting started, it didn't appear the least bit unprofessional.

"Thanks, fellas," I said as Tori and three other familiar faces greeted us.

"Oh my gosh, it really is Hope," one of the women said, hurrying over to give me an uncomfortable hug. It was Sharron, an old acquaintance from my high school days. The other two, Ted and Bonnie, I knew only in passing.

Sharron was so gleeful to see an old familiar face that she stood in the corner with me while I sorted through my materials, wanting to hear about my time in Bali and LA. As the Revival team were presenting first, I organized presentation materials so I would be able to set up quickly, while I told Sharron everything her nosey heart wanted to hear. "Oh, the beaches are nice in LA, but nothing compared to Bali."

Dustin cleared his throat.

"Sharron, we're ready to get started," he said, looking irritated at how friendly his fellow committee member was.

Dustin and the other committee members seated themselves at one end of a long table, looking out at the Revival team and at me. I took the chair in the corner near where Sharron and I had been chatting. The gentleman set up a large easel, sitting a covered picture atop it for the big reveal.

"Ladies and gentleman," Adam began. "Thank you so much for inviting us here today. We're very excited to present Revival's latest design to your town's committee, and we strongly believe you are going to see the benefit of hiring a company with over forty years' experience specific to the revitalization of small-town life."

I wrang my wrists. The competition was no laughing matter. The committee were ready to take notes. Sharron cracked open a water bottle as Adam continued his spiel about the company. The big reveal came as Bradley whipped the large black cloth away from the posterboard, and Sharron nearly choked on her water.

"What the heck is that?" Tori questioned bluntly. "Where's the clocktower?"

I'd been so focused on gaging the reactions of the committee that I hadn't even looked. I turned my head, and I gasped. What I saw was indeed a beautiful design, but it was not Golden. At least, not the Golden I knew. They must be joking! I stared at the strip mall, the large theater, and the miner statue, all which had been moved away from the center of town as though they were some second thought. The focus was no longer the clocktower but rather, a modern water fountain surrounded by an absurdly large roundabout and walk paths.

Sonny cleared his throat. "Now, before you get too shocked by what we're proposing, just know we're estimating a huge rate of return for what this new commercial center would bring to your town. Bradley's passing out some of our spec sheets on what Revival estimates on the profits Golden could make with the influx of tourists."

"Not to mention," Adam added, "this new design includes a significant amount of recycled material. Going green is in."

I snorted, and Adam shot me a look. I looked at my fingernails to avoid his gaze, but I caught Tori grinning in my direction.

Tori shook her head when Bradley reached her, not even wanting to take a sheet. "We didn't ask you to come in and bulldoze half our town," she said. "We wanted a bid on updating the clocktower, museum, and miner statue."

Dustin took Tori's sheet for her and placed it in front of her. "Before you all get upset with Revival, I should probably admit my part in this," Dustin said, opening his briefcase. He handed papers to the other committee members. "This is the preliminary inspection report on the clocktower which you will see has been deemed potentially unsafe. You all know we had to close it to the public last year due to a leak, and it's yet to open again, except for those working on the clock. It's been a nightmare. While it's completely possible for the structure to be reinforced and brought back up to the code, I personally don't see the point."

"Dustin," Ted muttered. "That clocktower holds a lot of value."

"What value?" Dustin questioned.

"Of the sentimental sort," Ted said. "You know how this town is."

"I swear, Ted, if you start with that old superstition—"

"He's right, Dustin," Sharron agreed. "Old town legend says Golden will only be prosperous for as long as the clocktower is running."

Dustin huffed. "I thought you were above that sort of nonsense, Sharron."

"I'm not one to jump on board with superstition," Bonnie said. "I'd like to hear exactly what Revival is proposing. That tower is an eyesore."

"Which is why we wanted to renovate it," Tori said.

"And the most financially forward mindset is a complete overhaul of our town center that a group like Revival could do in record time," Dustin said.

I cringed and bit my lip. The committee seemed divided. Ted and Tori were eager to end Revival's proposal for wanting to demolish half the town center. Dustin was clearly the idea man behind it, and Bonnie looked intrigued by the possibility. Sharron was harder to read as she remained silent, studying the charts.

For the next half hour, I sat in silence, listening to these men talk about the ridiculous expense of such a venture that the little town of Golden likely could not swing. But I had to admit they did really know what they were doing. They put in a bid just over the initial budget the committee had given them to work with; they knew they'd be able to squeeze more out of them later if needed. Their plan called for a completely new building for the museum, rezoning of current shops, new roads, and no more clocktower.

It made my skin crawl.

And the worst part of it was they seemed to be winning over the other committee members.

"We truly appreciate the time and effort you've put into this," Tori said. "But we do have another company here, and we'd like to hear from them before we go into deliberation."

The gentleman stepped aside, smiling happily at how well their pitch had gone while I made my way to the front.

I set up my own easel, bypassing the dramatic big reveal and propping up my large posterboard concept. Sharron smiled and, one by one, smiles crept on everyone's faces apart from Dustin's.

I cleared my throat. "As a Golden native, I know how important history is to this town. The clocktower especially. I can recall numerous fun evenings spent there as a teenager for various fall festivals and art shows. I was sad to hear it's been closed to the public for so long, but I'm thrilled at the possibility of working alongside you to restore it to full health. I have worked with a lot of commercial shopping centers in LA, and I understand Revival's thought, but I must argue there is still value in the historical significance of these precious sites."

"What have added to the tower, Hope?" Bonnie asked. "Did you extend the building?"

"Yes," I began. "In addition to updating the tower itself, giving it fresh paint and a new color scheme, new roofing, new shingles, and bringing it back up to code, I thought to add a small recreational area that could be accessed at the entrance." I handed packets to each of the committee members, avoiding eye contact with Dustin.

"This is going to be the largest expense, but I truly believe it's worth it," I continued. "Here, we can have a new public event space that incorporates an additional bit of our town's history. I've been in touch with the old minister of St. Mary's Cathedral. It burned down nine years ago, but a number of the pews were saved. The current owners are willing to donate them to be used as part of the interior décor."

"Oh, wow!" Ted said, excited by the design sketch I had on the third page of my pamphlet.

"My goal is to bring as much of that small town charm out as possible. You'll see on page six I've printed out some of the paintings currently on display at the museum. Ones I believe could be moved for décor in the new event center, placed behind glass displays, those specific to the clocktower and the church out town lost."

"Hey, that's my grandfather," Sharron said, pointing at one of the old portraits. "The museum's had that thing in storage instead of on display for years now."

"Yes," I said. "And while my plan for the museum does have a small extension, I wanted to spread that town history to the clocktower as well. There's a lot of value to maintaining historically important locations."

"Yes," Dustin said. "But the influx we'd get from the shopping center concept is much more impressive."

"I don't know, Dustin," Ted muttered. "Hope's research is showing a good number of benefits as well... and there's a lot less financial risk here, if I might add."

The committee members whispered between themselves as I continued. I showed them my design ideas for the museum as well as for the area surrounding the miner statue which included putting in a gazebo and picnic area. Dustin argued at every turn; he was clearly hoping on Revival stealing the show, and he seemed thrown off at how solid a plan I had.

At the end of the meeting, I was glad I'd come. Knowing the other architectural group wanted to demolish half my hometown's historical district had stirred something inside me. The anxiety of being back cascaded off me, and it was replaced with a newfound vigor.

Not my town, I thought with bitter resentment building.

# Chapter Four

Not surprisingly, the men from Revival were not as friendly come the end of the meeting. Sonny kindly offered to help me pack up my things, but he couldn't convince his coworkers to offer any assistance. They busied themselves with straightening their paperwork and meandering out into the hallway.

"You don't have to help me carry all this out to my car," I said.

He grinned. "I don't mind. They're just mad because you killed it." H folded up my easel and following me into the hallway.

"You're just saying that," I said. "A full restoration was a pretty big proposal, though, and I'm pretty sure the committee knew you guys were undershooting it when you pitched that budget."

"That's all part of the negotiation," Sonny said, opening the front door of the building to let me out first.

"Such a gentleman," I said. "Thanks."

"But you're probably right. We might have scared them."

"Your research was really solid," I said. "Truthfully, it would bring in a lot of revenue for the town, and I think the committee saw that right away. Not sure if I have much of a shot."

"I don't know," he said. "You just might. Half of them seemed stubborn about keeping that clocktower especially. I told Adam we should have left that in the design, but I'm the go-fetch-the-coffee guy of the group."

"Nice." I popped the back of my car open, thanking Sonny again for his politeness. It made Revival seem less like some big giant I had to conquer. They were just normal people like me, just with a big name attached. He set the easel down and trotted off to meet his companions; they had remained behind, likely trying to woo the committee.

I wasn't one to grovel, but I caught myself lingering, and I wondered if I should hold back to chat with some of the skeptics too. I was sure I had zero chance of convincing Dustin. He had been dead set against me the moment he'd spotted me in the grocery store, and he was ready to counter everything I had to say.

"Hope!" Tori hurried toward me, waving her arms excitedly.

I acknowledged her with a smile. "So, what's the damage? Is the whole committee bidding on Revival?"

"It's pretty split," Tori admitted. "Ted and Bonnie are undecided. Dustin's obviously all for Revival. But I think you've got Sharron on your side."

"Be straight with me. What are the chances I can swing Ted and Bonnie?"

"Honestly, I think Dustin's got Bonnie convinced to go with Revival," Tori said.

"So, Ted's going to be our swing vote," I muttered. "He seemed pretty adamant about keeping that clocktower."

"His concern is kind of legitimate though," Tori said. "He was all for your design until he started looking at that preliminary inspection report. He's worried fixing the tower's going to be a money pit."

"I'm curious about that inspection report," I said.

A man cleared his throat behind me, and I spun around to see Dustin.

He chuckled at my surprise. "What are you curious about, Hope?" he asked, retrieving his car keys from his pocket and rattling them.

"It just seemed vague is all," I explained. "I'm not accusing anyone of mishandling it; I just was thinking about heading over to the clocktower myself and checking it out. Seeing the damage for myself."

"Are you serious?" Dustin questioned. "Why would you do that? It's all in the report."

"Like I said, the report was a little vague."

"I have a key," Tori said. "Wanna go now? We can snag some lunch in town."

I cringed at the thought of going to lunch, but I knew I needed to get it over sooner rather than later. "Great idea!"

"That tower is closed to the public," Dustin said.

"Yeah, but as a committee member, I'm not the public," Tori snapped. "Would you relax, Dustin? Act like an adult. This is a business exchange. Get over your little high school nonsense."

Dustin's jaw fell open. "You are unbelievable," he snarled.

"You're just trying to push Hope out because she dumped you when you were kids. That's why you can't see the value in what she's brining to the table," Tori said.

I felt like crawling into a hole. Sometimes Tori's idea of helping was drastically different from mine.

Dustin puffed up. "You think I'm bitter over a high-school breakup? That was close to twenty years ago!"

"After the way you acted in that committee meeting, it certainly looks like that," Tori said.

Dustin threw his head back and turned on his heels. "I can't believe you think that little of me, Tori," he said. "You too, Hope."

"I didn't say a thing," I muttered. "But to be fair, you haven't exactly been welcoming."

He turned around, glaring at us. "Did you ever think that seeing you just makes me think of him?" he questioned, and my chest tightened. "Get over yourself, Hope. You're not the one that got away. You're just the one who let Steven go out to the river that day when he had no business—"

"Out of line!" Tori shouted, cutting him off. "That was way out of line, and you know it!"

Dustin's expression softened; he exhaled deeply. "I'm sorry," he said, and he hurried to his car without another word.

I blinked away the tears burning my eyes and attempted to shake off the exchange. "Well, that was… not what I expected."

"Forget him, and I'm sorry. I should have kept my mouth shut," Tori said. "Clearly he's dealing with a lot more than I thought. I'm sorry, Hope."

"I appreciate you trying to back me up," I said. "But let's not poke the bear again, all right?"

"Yes ma'am! So, you still want to go to the tower? I have a bit of time before I have to pick up the kids," Tori said.

"Absolutely."

We jumped into my car and headed toward the clocktower. It stood near the town's center, a large grass area surrounding it with cracked walkways. I instantly was thrown back in time.

My first kiss with Steven, his face so close to mine. His breath on my neck, his arms wrapped around me so tightly I could barely breathe.

Time had stopped that night. Here at the clocktower.

Now, I looked around at the front stoop covered in a layer of grime.

Hmmm. Nothing a good pressure washer couldn't take care of.

Some of the windows in the tower were cracked, some too filthy to even see through, but the memories were here. The sentiment was here.

"How can Dustin want to tear this place down?"

"I don't know," Tori said, staring up at the clock. "He told me his old man brought him here when he was just a kid, throwing a ball around. He learned how to catch on this very lawn, he said."

"I doubt there's a single person in Golden who doesn't have some memory attached to this place," I said. "It's just so weird the way Dustin's acting… so callous about it."

"I don't think he's being callous necessarily," Tori said, reaching into her purse. "I think he's just ready for a fresh start and wants the rest of the town to head there with him. But we're Golden people, and we like our traditions." She pulled out a key and twirled it around before sticking it into the lock.

My nose instantly tickled from the dust as we entered. "Geeze, when you said this place had been closed for a while, I didn't think it meant no one had been taking care of it."

"Hold on, lights should still be working. We can see how bad the damage is," Tori said. She flicked the switch. The light flashed for a second before the bulb burst, making us both cry out.

Our screams turned to laughter.

"Ooh, that's a bad sign," I said, looking around. I pulled out my phone, turned on its flashlight, and walked towards the enormous staircase. "I see one of the leaks over here by the steps. Little bit of water damage, but it's totally fixable." I assessed each nook and cranny as I walked.

Tori followed close behind, her phone light on as well. "More windows wouldn't be such a bad idea—or at least clean ones."

"Stained glass would be possible if we could stay under budget elsewhere," I said. "Would add a nice touch, don't you think?"

"Especially in this stairwell. Those old windows don't let in enough light," Tori said as we rounded the corner.

Something snagged my foot, and I fell, letting out a surprised shriek. My phone skittered away, and I caught myself on the upper steps.

"Ack! What was that!" I exclaimed. As I stood, I caught the horror in Tori's eyes.

I glanced down and yelped, jumping back several steps. A man was sprawled out, his head bashed and bloodied. "Tori!" I shrieked. "Call 911!"

Tori knelt down by the man. "Hope, he's long dead," she said. "Look at this... this blood. It's dried up."

"Please don't tell me," I said, my heart beating faster by the second. "Please don't tell me we just found a body in the clocktower."

# Chapter Five

Dread washed over me.

A body in the clocktower?

"Do you know him?" I asked.

Tori shook her head and looked down at the phone. "No network. Let's get out of here and call 911."

We rushed out of the tower. While Tori dialed the police, I tried to process the shock.

My ears throbbed as pressure built between my temples. All I could hear was my own heartbeat and a distant shrill from Tori.

A body! We'd found a body inside the clocktower, and from the looks of things, he'd been there a few hours.

Maybe a day?

I wondered how much he'd suffered. From the odd angle of his body, he looked like he might have broken his neck.

Did he fall down the stairs or something?

"Hope..." I snapped to attention.

"The police are on their way. They said for us to wait out front," Tori said. "And for me to lock up the clocktower and not let anyone inside."

"I can't believe this, Tori."

"Me either," she said, checking the time on her phone. "I need to call my husband. Someone's got to pick Nolan up, and it doesn't look like I'm going to make it."

I stood aside as she made the call, the image of that poor man imprinted in my mind. I waited in perfect stillness until I heard sirens. Two patrol cars pulled up, and Tori and I headed that way without saying a word to one another. Three officers stepped out, and the eldest one came forward.

"Are you the one who made the 911 call?" he asked.

"Yes, that was me," Tori said, still sounding flustered. "We found a body in the clocktower."

The officers followed us back to the clocktower, asking questions. "When did you find it? And what were you ladies doing here?" the oldest man asked. He turned to his companions. "Make sure paramedics are en route."

"Yes, sir," one said, making the call to dispatch on his radio.

"Stay out here, ladies," the younger officer said, and he and the older one hurried inside.

"This is crazy," I managed to say. The third officer meandered up to us, a paper and pen at the ready to take our statements.

"Ladies, I'm Officer Barney Stent," he began. "I have a few questions. To start, what are you doing here? This clocktower is shut to the public."

"I just finished proposing a remodeling project regarding the tower to the town council," I said. "Tori's on the committee, and we came to follow up on an inspection report. She has a key to the building, and we wanted to take a look at a few things that had been brought up in the report. That's when we saw the man lying in the middle of the stairs."

"Do you know him personally?" Officer Stent asked.

"I didn't recognize him," I said, and I glanced Tori's way.

She shrugged. "Honestly, I'm not sure. I was so flabbergasted by it... I checked his pulse, but I didn't pay much attention to his features. He kind of looked familiar, I think, but I couldn't tell you who he was."

"Officer Edward Bucks," the older officer said as he exited the tower, joining us at the stoop. "I'm afraid there's nothing we can do for him. Stent, are the paramedics on their way??"

"Yeah," Officer Stent said. "Coroner too."

"Go around and make sure all the entrances to the tower are locked," Officer Bucks said. "This is now an active crime scene."

"A crime scene?" I asked. "But he just fell down the stairs!"

Officer Bucks removed his hat. "I don't think so, ladies," he said. "Noticed some bruising around the man's neck that look suspiciously like handprints. I believe he was pushed."

"You're kidding," Tori said, her mouth gaping open. "Do you know who he is? Or was..."

Officer Bucks didn't answer. "Get a move on," he snapped at the younger officers, and they hurried around the building. He turned back to us. "Did Stent get your statements?"

"He started to," Tori said. "And I'm sorry, but you didn't answer my question, sir. Do you know who that is in there?"

He sighed and held up a wallet. "Yeah, he had his identification on him," he said, flipping it open. "Wayne Maloney."

"Oh!" Tori yelped, and I looked at her curiously.

"You know him?" I asked.

"Well, no, not personally," Tori said. "But I know I've heard the name. He's working at E-Goldrush.com. Like an intern or something. Kind of new to town. I think Dustin knows him."

"Dustin?" I questioned. Officer Bucks didn't pay us any mind. Instead, he walked to his patrol car, opened the truck and rummaged through it.

Tori hugged herself. "I remember the name being mentioned. I think maybe Dustin's aunt knows Wayne somehow."

"Probably through the goldmines," I said "Dustin's father owns one of the mines outside town. They're all pretty tight in those circles."

"That's probably it," Tori agreed.

Officer Bucks made his way back to us. He had crime scene tape at the ready, just as the ambulance pulled up. Tori and I stepped aside, not sure whether they'd want to speak to us again. We sat on an old, decrepit bench that was along the path, watching the officers putting up crime scene tape and speaking with crime scene unit.

"This is the craziest thing I've ever seen happen in Golden," Tori said.

Why didn't Dustin want us to come to the tower?

It seemed too coincidental, but almost as soon as the thought occurred, I chased it away. Sure, Dustin and I had not exactly been the best of friends in recent years. Heck, we'd not spoken once since I left Golden after Steven passed, and we were hardly speaking before then. But just because we weren't on the good terms didn't make him some monster.

I chewed my nails. I thought I'd kicked that habit long ago, but apparently it was back. Something felt wrong. I thought back to my interaction with Dustin in the parking lot outside city hall. He'd been so angry—angry enough to suggest I had something to do with Steven's death. The knot in my stomach tightened. It wasn't like I hadn't thought that before; I knew the waters were high that day Steven went out.

I knew it'd been a bad idea, but I'd kept my mouth shut.

Was Dustin really holding onto that sort of anger? And if so, what else could he be angry about? People who've zeroed in that kind of anger tend to find other things to fuel their anger.

Could this Wayne character have done something that pushed Dustin over the edge?

You stop that right now! I scolded myself as Tori nudged me.

"Look who's here," she said, nodding toward the parking lot. Several emergency vehicles and witnesses made a b-line for the clocktower. People are nosey, especially people in small towns with nothing better to do.

I scanned the parking lot for what Tori pointed out. Dustin's car pulled into a parking space. I frowned.

Returning to the crime scene? I pondered with disgust.

Were my feelings so bitter about Dustin that I could make up he had anything to do with this? I tried to shake it off, but I couldn't.

He stepped out of his car, looking puzzled. Was he faking it, or was he seriously not aware of what was going on at the clocktower? Then he spotted Tori and me, and I couldn't read his expression. Was it relief? But he quickly soured up, and his expression changed to annoyance as he slammed his car door.

# Chapter Six

"What is he even doing here?" Tori hissed. She was probably still irate about our conversation outside city hall. I was too, but after what we had found in the clocktower, I'd moved on. Plus, guilt pinched in my chest now for of the thoughts that had been running through my head about Dustin.

I knew Dustin.

And I knew he was no killer.

So why would I think such a thing, even if only for a second?

He didn't bother walking along the path leading up to the clocktower; instead, he cut through the lawn directly toward us. He stared intensively and instinctually, we stood up.

"Dustin, what are you doing here?" I asked.

"I saw the ambulances," he said. "And the patrol cars. I knew you two were here..." His voice trailed off, and he quickly hid the worried expression. "What happened?"

So he'd come to make sure we were all right.

But he clearly didn't want to show he'd had a moment of sympathy for us.

"We came here to follow up on that inspection report you showed us," Tori explained. "And there was a body in the stairwell."

"What!" he asked, stunned.

I studied his reaction. I'd read that it's hard to fake shock, and Dustin was hardly an actor. He looked legitimately surprised.

"Yeah," Tori said. "There was a guy. Looks like he fell down the stairs and hit his head, but the cops think there was a fight or something. Do you know someone named Wayne Maloney? I think I've heard you mention the name before."

"Wait, it's Wayne?" Dustin asked, wide-eyed. "That's who you found? He's dead?"

"So, you do know him?" I asked.

"I mean, sort of," he said, straightening himself. "I don't know him personally, but that's the guy renting the upstairs room at my aunt's house."

"Aunt Laverne?" That was Dustin's aunt who had a large upstairs loft. She'd had a few tenants over the years. Steven had even rented it once, fresh out of high school and before the two of us got together. "How is Laverne?" I asked. "Oh my goodness, I've missed her so much!"

"Yeah, she's fine," he said. "I wouldn't have even known the guy's name if it wasn't for what happened yesterday."

"What happened yesterday?" I asked.

"He wasn't paying rent, so she had him evicted," Dustin explained. "Aunt Laverne asked me to swing to make sure it went smoothly. She can handle herself, but you never know how people are going to react to something like that."

"How did he react?" Tori asked. "Did he cause a scene?"

"No, not really," Dustin said. "It's just crazy. I saw him yesterday morning, but that was the first and last time I saw the guy. He knew it was coming. My aunt warned him a few times that if he didn't pay rent, he would have to go. He took half his stuff and said he'd be back for the rest over the weekend. Seemed pretty understanding of the situation."

"You might want to talk to the police, Dustin," I said. "If they're thinking murder, they're going to want to piece together his last few hours. For all we know, you might be the last person who saw him alive."

"I didn't think about that," Dustin said, looking green in the face at the thought of getting involved with a homicide investigation, but an officer was already walking over.

Officer Bucks looked bothered. "Sir, we're taping this area off. These ladies are witnesses, and I'm going to have to ask you to get behind—"

"He knows Wayne," Tori said. "Says he saw him yesterday."

Dustin scowled.

Was he just going to leave without saying anything to the police?

"Did you, now?" Officer Bucks asked. "Dustin, right?"

"Yes, sir," Dustin said. "Dustin Peterson."

"I thought so. You're George's kid," he said. "You're saying you know our victim?"

"Is this really a homicide?" Dustin asked.

"Looks that way to me, but I'm not CSI." Officer Bucks dug around in his pocket, pulling out a small notepad. "Dustin Peterson, when did you last see Wayne?"

"Yesterday morning," he said. "He was leaving my aunt's. She'd been renting him a room for a while, and I was there to see him out."

"See him out?" Bucks questioned.

"He wasn't paying his rent," Dustin said. "Nothing happened. He took his stuff and left. Hardly said a word."

The officer looked Dustin up and down, then frowned. He made a note in his book and muttered, "I see."

I glanced in Tori's direction. She had a look of concern on her face as she watched the exchange.

After taking Dustin's statement and contact information, Officer Bucks wandered back to the crime scene. "You ladies are good to go," he said over his shoulder, as though it was a passing thought.

Dustin eyed Tori sharply. "What are you trying to pull, Tori?"

"I just thought it might be useful information," she said, holding up both hands defensively. "I'm sorry. I didn't mean to make it look like I was accusing you of anything."

"This is the last thing I need right now," Dustin said. "I've got a lot on my plate, Tori. I don't need to be dragged around by the police, answering a bunch of questions about a guy I barely know."

Tori huffed. I could tell she wanted to pop back at him, but she resisted. They had been working together on the board for a while now. I couldn't help but wonder if their relationship had been strained the entire time, or if the tension was thanks to my reappearance.

"Well, we should probably get out of here," I said, nudging Tori. "We didn't mean to get you involved, Dustin, but you did come walking up to the crime scene. You can't really blame us."

Dustin scowled. "Yeah, Next time I see a bunch of ambulances, I'll just assume everything's fine." And, with that, he stormed off.

I exhaled. A sting of guilt pierced me rather hard. He had actually been worried about us, and now Tori's comment had managed to get the police on his tail. Even as we made our way to the parking lot ourselves, keeping our distance so as not to catch up with Dustin, we saw an officer hurry to stop him. We were too far back to hear what is being said, but it was clear they didn't want him to leave just yet.

"Shoot," Tori muttered as we climbed into my car. "I really didn't mean to make things difficult on him. You don't think I got Dustin in trouble, do you?"

"I'm not sure," I said. I gripped the steering wheel. Now, there were two officers and a CSI standing around Dustin. I wished I could hear what was being said, but it looked like Dustin was doing a good job at remaining cooperative. He looked like he was just trying to help, but by the way he had spoken to Tori and me, I knew he was fuming on the inside.

"I know you were just trying to help."

"Exactly," Tori said. "I thought he could help with the investigation. For all we know, Dustin and his aunt were the last ones to see Wayne alive."

I watched Dustin's exchange with the officers, feeling I couldn't drive away while they kept him. Eventually, he shook hands with one of the officers, passed him a business card, and climbed into his own car.

Tori and I both exhaled in relief, glad we hadn't gotten Dustin into trouble. Finally feeling comfortable to pull out, and we headed back in the direction of city hall so I could return Tori to her car.

"This is all pretty intense," Tori said. "I didn't notice any bruising around the guy's neck. Do you really think someone might have killed him?"

"Maybe," I said. "I'm still trying to figure out what an E-Goldrush intern was doing in an abandoned clocktower."

We grew quiet as I pulled up at city hall. There was something Tori wanted to say, and I was pretty sure I knew what it is. "What is it?" I asked.

She crossed her arms, looking uncomfortable. "It's just... do you think Dustin could have had something to do with this? I mean, think about it. He sure was hellbent on wanting that tower torn down, right? It would be an easy way to make sure the body wasn't discovered. And he flat-out admitted being with Wayne yesterday. What if their interaction yesterday wasn't as civil as Dustin suggested?"

"Wow," I said. "Come on, Tori, you really think Dustin could have killed someone?"

"Not on purpose! I mean...well, what if they argued and...I know, it's a little crazy," she admitted. "And maybe I'm just worked up from the whole ordeal. Dustin's not a bad guy, but he does have a reputation for being temperamental. I mean, I think I believe he really was just pulling up to the clocktower because he knew we were there and saw the ambulances."

I smiled. He'd been worried about us. Maybe there was hope that the two of us would be able to get along through the renovation projects, after all. "I think we might be jumping the gun. I'm not going to lie, the same thought did cross my mind too, Tori. But you and I both know Dustin well enough to say that it's utter nonsense."

"You're right," she said. "He just made me mad right before... you know, we found a body. I guess my brain is connecting the two. It's terrible of me to even think that of him. But, wow, a murder in Golden! My husband is going to have a fit when I tell him about this."

"Might want to tell him to keep it under wraps," I said. "Nothing's official yet. It was just that one cop who seemed to think there was foul play involved. We don't know what the official police statement is going to say."

"Yeah, you're right," she said, shaking her head. "I better get going. Nolan is probably already giving him a run for his money. I'll catch you later, Hope." She opened the car door and climbed out, sticking her head back in for a final thought. "You did great today, by the way. I really think you've got a good shot. Everyone loved your presentation—even Dustin, I think. Not that he's ever going to admit that." She winked, and I thanked her as she closed the door and strutted away.

I gripped the steering wheel, having a hard time wrapping my brain around everything that had taken place in the last few hours. My first week back at Golden was already getting to me, understandably so after what we found in that clocktower.

As I drove anxiously back to the motel I couldn't let go of the thought that a man had died in Golden's beautiful clocktower. Poor man.

And then the other more selfish thought.

What would this mean for the renovation project?

# Chapter Seven

Four.

That was the absurd number of people I bumped into that morning who immediately recognized me and forced me to have awkward conversations about my long absence and abrupt return. That's what I get for venturing too close to Golden's town center for breakfast.

I'd had a boost of confidence that morning; the memory of the previous day's proposal was still fresh on my mind. The more I thought about it, the more I realized I'd completely slayed it. Sure, Revival had some experience points on me and all, but even those Dustin attempted to win over seemed hesitant toward their concepts. It was that boost of confidence that now had me sitting outside one of Golden's oldest cafés, enjoying a breakfast tart with a newspaper, looking through the classifieds for a potential rental.

"So good to see you again, Hope," the server said as she handed me my coffee.

"Thanks, you too," I said. I picked up my mug and took a sip of the piping hot drink. The server was number four on the list of people who had recognized me that morning. A lot of people were going to be curious about what I had been up to in the past five years. And, if I was going to hang around for a while, I didn't want to rub people the wrong way by telling them it was none of their business. I needed to get used to this.

While eating breakfast, I flipped through the newspaper, circling ads for rooms for rent. There weren't a lot of options. And the few that were there seemed overpriced or too far from where I would be working. I sighed, closing the newspaper I glimpsed the front cover. It was a photograph of the clocktower. The discovery of the body had made the front page.

How had I missed it?

"Oh no," I grumbled, realizing my and Tori's faces were right there on the front cover as well, standing outside the clocktower with one of the officers. Everyone in Golden knew I was back now. "You have got to be kidding me," I said, skimming the article. It even mentioned me by name as one of the people to have discovered the body. "No, no, no, and no..." My stomach formed knots.

The paper was online too. The story was probably being shared all over the place.

As I panicked about my face being on the cover of the story, a particular line in the article caught my eye. Regrettable accident...

"What?" I took the time to read the entire article.

Late yesterday afternoon, local residences Hope Wilson and Tori Kemp found a body within Golden's famous clocktower. The two ladies immediately called 911, and the man was pronounced dead on the scene. The name of the unfortunate victim has not yet been released to the public and won't be until police have contacted the loved ones of the deceased. The deceased, according to police investigators, fell down the stairwell in the clocktower, which resulted in a cracked skull and loss of consciousness. Unfortunately, as the deceased was alone during the incident, help didn't arrive in time to save him. This regrettable accident is drawing new concerns from residences about the safety of the decaying tower. Yesterday, a mere hour before the body's discovery, Golden's renovation committee met to hear two separate proposals for the towns famous clocktower, and we are still awaiting the committee's decision. One cannot help but speculate whether or not the incident will affect the committee's decision.

I stopped reading.

Why was the article calling this an accident, when Officer Bucks had said there were marks around the guy's neck that seemed to suggest there had been some sort of struggle? I couldn't wrap my brain around this conflicting information. It waspolice didn't want anyone to panic. Or maybe the article writer simply didn't do his due diligence. Either way, the article left me unsettled.

"Hope Wilson!" I jump at the shrieking voice, preparing myself to be bombarded by yet another familiar face.

Looking up, I saw someone I actually didn't mind seeing. An older woman with graying hair, pulled back in a bun and stuffed full of brightly colored clips, stared back at me. She walked with a bright cane, dressed in walking shoes and loose-fitting runner's attire.

"Aunt Laverne!" I exclaimed, surprised to see Dustin's aunt out walking. I jumped up and greeted her.

The older woman threw her arms around my neck, cooing at me. "Dustin told me you were back in town!" she exclaimed. "Oh, I'm so glad. So glad!"

Laverne Peterson was a lively woman. She'd always had more energy than someone her half her age. In some ways, she was everyone's grandma, giving the youngsters sweets all the time, and in others she constantly defied the stereotypes, like her collection of antique pickaxes. Everyone from high school loved her. We had all adored Aunt Laverne and her charismatic charm and when I left, she remained in my heart even as the rest of Golden faded away.

"It's… good to be back," I said, not telling her I had mixed feelings about my return.

"Do you mind?" she asked, gesturing toward my table.

I smiled. "Not at all."

We sat down together, and she beamed across at me. "How have you been, darling?" she asks once she'd settled.

"Doing well," I said. "Been really busy."

"Dustin tells me you're placing a bid for the clocktower redesign?"

"That's right," I said, and my cheeks flushed. "I hope he didn't give you too much of an earful?"

She laughed. "I know, he's bidding on that other group. What is it, Renewal or something?"

I started to correct her, but her wry grin of hers I knew she said the name incorrectly on purpose. I laughed as well. "You haven't changed much," I told her. "It's really good to see you, Aunt Laverne. The cane is new. Is everything all right?"

She huffed at me. "Everyone always so worried about me. I'm not that old, you know! But as soon as you break a hip, everybody's got you pegged for a granny. I tripped going down the stairs about a year ago, now this stupid hip of mine has me feeling older than I actually am."

"You tripped going down the stairs?" For a split second, I imagined Wayne Maloney in the stairwell, and I shuddered.

"Just missed a step right at the bottom," she said. "Not like I went tumbling down or anything. Landed wrong. Are you all right, Hope?"

"I'm fine," I said.

She exhaled and then pointed at the paper. "Saw that article this morning. Looks like you've been busy since you got back. Dustin tells me the unnamed man was my old tenant, Wayne. Is that true?"

I nodded. "I don't think we were supposed to share that information, though."

"No, but Dustin was going to have to tell me eventually. Wayne was supposed to come get the rest of his belongings from me before the weekend. It's a real shame. He was a nice young man, that Wayne," she said. "If it wasn't for the little issue of rent, I would have enjoyed having him around a while longer."

"Were things civil when he left?" I asked. "Dustin said he was there when you were giving him the boot."

"For backup only," she said reassuringly. "The busted hip has slowed me down a bit, but I can still put up a fight." Laverne held up both hands into fists, nearly letting her cane roll out of her lap in the process. We both laughed. "Gracious…" she says. "There I go showing off."

"I've really missed you," I said with absolute honesty. There were plenty of things I'd missed about Golden, and Aunt Laverne was definitely in the top ten. "I swear, every time I smelled butterscotch, I'd think of you."

She smiled wildly. "Oh, that's right. You always were partial to my butterscotch buttons, weren't you?"

"I love butterscotch," I said. "Do you still do those hand-crafted candies?"

"Of course!" she exclaimed. "The hip hasn't slowed me down that much. The Butter and Egg Parade is coming up, so I've been going at it for the past several days. I think this is the first time I've been out of the house all week."

Old memories flashed through my mind. I'd forgotten about the parade. It was a big celebration of Golden's agricultural history; Steven and I'd had a number of dates to the annual festival. Heck, even Dustin and I had gone to it together back in high school. "Wow, that is coming up, isn't it?" I said, doing my best to keep the sadness from my voice.

"All those candies," she said with a heavy sigh. "It takes me forever to wrap them. That's the real challenge. Every single one needs to be individually wrapped. My back gets tired."

"What sort are you doing this year?" I asked.

"Let's see…" she began, "hand-crafted vanilla caramel cremes, the butterscotch buttons you love so much, jawbreakers, Dustin's favorites—those root beer barrels, and of course, honey roll midges…"

"Geeze! Sounds like you're keeping yourself busy," I said. "I'm glad you have such a fun hobby. I remember Dustin telling Steven and me how worried he was about you when you retired. Said he was worried you were going to get bored… Laverne?" She had totally tuned me out. Her eyes rested on the newspaper, which she promptly snatched up.

"What are you circling?" she asked, as nosey as I remembered her being.

"Hey!" I said, though I really shouldn't have been surprised. This was a pretty typical Aunt Laverne move.

"You're looking for a place to stay?" she asked, flipping through the newspaper and looking at all the different rentals I had circled.

"Well, yes," I said. "If I get the job, I'm going to need a place to stay. The restoration project will be an ongoing thing. It'll take at least a year, if not more. So I need—"

"Come stay with me!" she said, wide eyed.

I chuckled. "I'm sorry?"

"You heard me," she said. "You said yourself I'm out a tenant. My upstairs is quite spacious, just what you would need for a temporary setup. Plus, I could use some youthful hands to help me wrap all those sweets!"

Dustin would kill me, I thought with a hint of amusement.

"I don't know," I said. "I wouldn't want to overstep. I'm sure you know Dustin and I are not exactly on the best of terms."

"All the more reason for you to do it," she said with a wink.

"You're terrible!" I couldn't help but to laugh. "Gosh, I've really missed you."

"Why don't you come by today and look at the room?" she suggested. "It still has some of Wayne's belongings that are going to need to be moved out, but other than that the place is move-in ready. You remember where I live, don't you? It's right down the road from the clocktower. Walking distance. Can't beat that if that's where you're going to be working. Just a short drive to city hall, too."

She was right—the location was perfect. It was right down the road from town square. It wouldn't take me five minutes to get to city hall by car, and I could walk to the clocktower, museum, and even the miner statue.

"You know what?" I said. "I think I will come check it out. I can't make any promises just yet, though. If I don't get the bid, I'll be heading back to Los Angeles. I'd hate for you to put all your hopes in me renting your place and then for it to fall through."

"Honey," Laverne said. "I'll be happy because I'll get to catch up with you. I always liked you, and I would love to have you stay."

# Chapter Eight

Aunt Laverne's place brought back a lot of memories. She'd been very involved in Dustin's life growing up, the fun, silly adult in our lives who threw house parties for his friends. Walking up the drive alongside her was like taking a step back in time. The large front lawn was covered in various flowers, out of season yet somehow blooming perfectly.

I paused halfway up the driveway, staring at the enormous oak tree with a little wooden swing. I could see myself sitting in that thing, fresh out of high school, while Steven pushed me and Dustin sulked.

"I remember when Steven lived here with you," I said. "Right after school."

That was another thing about this part of town that made me uneasy. Just down the road was the house Steven and I had called home for so long. It was a modest place we'd gotten a killer deal on when we were newlyweds. I made a mental note to never take the shortcut to downtown from here, lest I found myself driving right by that old house.

Laverne stopped walking. "You know, dear, if you think this might be too painful for you, I understand. Though I wouldn't mind seeing Dustin cringe when he finds out you're staying with me. He's gotten so stuffy lately. He needs a good wake up call."

I snorted. "You're terrible!"

"Of course I am," she said. "Now, come on in, and let's see if my butterscotch buttons have cooled before we go look at that room."

My mouth watered at the thought. She would have a bunch of butterscotch buttons sitting in her kitchen when I came to look at the spare room. I swear, it's like she ran into me on purpose, and knowing Aunt Laverne, that was entirely probable.

The wood paneling on the kitchen walls, painted bright yellow, dated the place back to the thirties. The kitchen had been updated back when I was a kid, so the large appliances seemed to burst forth from the walls next to the painfully narrow cabinets.

Spread across the kitchen's large island were various sweets, ready to be hand wrapped. She pushed a pan in my direction, and I could smell the butterscotch. I popped one in my mouth, and I swear I was seventeen again. How many times did I casually stroll by that house, hoping Aunt Laverne had a fresh batch of these things to offer?

"Oh, my goodness, so good," I said. "I've been craving these things for five years now. That's an itch that really needed scratching."

"I miss you too, dear," she said, propping her cane up in a corner before sitting on a barstool, stretching her legs out. "You should have seen my doctor last visit. He was shocked at my rate of recovery. I always push myself, even at my age. Dustin has a fit whenever I tell him I've been out hiking again."

"He worries about you," I said, eyeing the butterscotch treats. Laverne laughed and pushed them even closer to me, so I popped another one into my mouth. "You really think you could handle me as a roommate, Aunt Laverne?"

She clasped her hands together. "Honey, of course, or I wouldn't have invited you over and enticed you with butterscotch. Now, let's go on upstairs and look at that room, and you can tell me what you think."

I walked behind Laverne, worried about how she was going to handle the stairs with her hip injury, but she did just fine. We entered the bedroom, the only room upstairs, and I looked around. The wooden paneling was there as well, painted a soft pink. The furniture, a queen-sized bed, matching dresser and chest of drawers, and two nightstands, were a pretty off-white. There was a private beach-themed bathroom that made me grin.

The room was bigger than I recalled, which was good. While talked prices, I realized she was giving me a wonderful deal. So, we shook on it. "Looks like I'm moving in," I said. "But, you know, I won't be here any more than a month if this bid falls through. Are you sure you want me taking up space if I wind up dipping out so soon?"

"Hope, I told you, I love your company no matter what," she said, and she waved her hand at the pile of boxes. "But if you're moving in, it's going to take some work. That's all Wayne's stuff—most of it, anyways. The drawers are still full. Not sure if he got to the end tables either. So, if you want the place, you'll have to bring all these boxes downstairs. His family will probably come by eventually and pick it all up."

"I see," I said, eyeing the boxes. I would save a lot of money if I moved in right away. Night rates on the motel room were adding up. I rolled up my sleeves and told her I was ready to work, and she clapped her hands gleefully.

"Wonderful!" she said. "I'll go print out a rental agreement while you get started on that."

"Where would you like me to put the boxes?" I asked.

"Dining room," she said, already making her way out the door.

"Will do," I said, and I grabbed the first boxes.

One by one, I took the boxes downstairs and placed them on her dining room table. There were about half a dozen boxes already full, and another four or five would need to be filled. I opened the chest of drawers and started pulling out Wayne's clothes.

It felt odd, going through his things. I didn't know Wayne, and I was digging through his clothes. I cringed as I came to the underwear drawer. Pulling the whole drawer out, I dumped its contents into an empty box. It was all clean, sure, but I wasn't about to mess with a dead guy's underwear. I slid the box across the floor with my foot and opened one of the end tables. There was a cluster of random items: movie ticket stubs, a deck of cards, some mix-matched socks, and some bank statements.

I had a tendency to be nosier than I should be, but I gave into temptation and perused the bank statements. That's when I saw a wire transfer of over twenty grand. "Wayne, you little punk! You had over twenty grand stashed away, and you couldn't pay Laverne her rent?" I asked as I flipped through. There was a second deposit, also a wire transfer, of over thirty thousand.

"What is this?" I stood up. Something didn't feel right about this. Both transfers happened within a week of Wayne's death.

Abandoning my cleaning up mission, I took the bank statements and headed downstairs. "Hey, Laverne, I'm going to run out for a bit. I'll be back to finish up and sign that rental agreement later," I called, and from the back of the house I heard the old woman tell me to lock the front door on the way out.

I hurried out, bank statements in hand, and made my way to the town's police station. I went to the front desk, where I asked to speak with Sheriff James Groth.

"He'll be back in a few minutes," the officer up front told me, so I sat on the bench in the lobby.

I didn't have to wait long. He soonstrutted through the front doors, arms loaded with two drink carriers which he plopped down on the front desk with a yawn. He took one of the drinks, and the officer at the desk pointed him in my direction. The sheriff beamed, and he headed toward me. "Hope Wilson," he sang. "I heard you were back in town. Back in town and already in trouble, too."

James and I went back. He went to my high school, a year behind me, and we ran in the same circles in those days. We had lost touch after high school, but he was among those to bid me farewell when I bolted after Steven's death. He even tried talking me out of leaving, rightfully assuming I was running from my problems.

"It's good to see you too, James," I said. "I heard you were sheriff now, but I didn't believe it."

"Ouch, my pride," he teased. "What can I do for you, Hope?"

I handed him the bank statements. "I was helping Aunt Laverne clear out Wayne Maloney's rental space. I'm renting the room for a while. Anyways, I found this while I was clearing out his drawers."

"What is it? A bank statement?" he asked, taking it from me and skimming it. "Hmmm…"

"Someone has been sending him a lot of money," I said. "Maybe it has something to do with his murder?"

"We've ruled his death an accident," James said. "Case is closed, Hope."

I frowned. "You're joking."

"No, I'm not," he said. "We have no reason to think he was killed. He just fell down the stairs."

"Officer Bucks said he saw abrasions on the guy's neck," I said "Like someone had tried strangling him."

"Yes," James said. "You're right about that, but those abrasions were old. Bruising had been there long before he took that tumble down the stairs. I pulled the kid's records, and he had gotten into a bar fight a couple of weeks ago. That's where the bruises on his neck came from. He was arrested for the brawl, and you can see the bruises in his mugshot."

"I don't know, James," I said. "I seriously doubt he just fell down the stairs. And besides, what was he even doing in the clocktower?"

"Who knows," he said. "But, we're not investigating a murder here."

"But what about these bank statements?" I questioned. "Don't you think that's a little suspicious?"

"Maybe," he said. "He wasn't paying his rent. Maybe someone he's friendly with sent him some money to help him out. Who really knows? Point is, this case is closed. So, make sure you put that back where you got it from and send it on to his family."

"James," I argued. "This is seriously messed up. Someone killed Wayne."

"No, they didn't," he said. "Besides, we've got a lot more to worry about around here than some intern taking a fall in a stairwell. We've got the Butter and Egg weekend celebration coming up, and—"

"Whoa," I said, interrupting. "Are you putting off a murder investigation because you're worried about tourist influx?"

"Hope!" he snapped at me. "You know me better than that. We don't have any real evidence to suggest this was murder, so we're wrapping it up. Sure, the town's economics are on the upswing, so sure, we have reason for wanting this thing wrapped up quickly, but that doesn't mean—"

"Save it, James," I said, shaking my head. "You've clearly made up your mind. And, you know what? Shame on you and anyone else who was involved in this decision." I turned, storming out of the station.

# Chapter Nine

The following day, I cleared out of the motel, packing my few suitcases into my car. Part of me really didn't want to move because I was worried about not getting the bid, but I knew it would save me a good chunk of cash. Worst case scenario was I wound up at Laverne's for a couple of weeks, helping her wrap some candies. It would be nice being downtown for a few weeks, too, instead of in a motel far outside the city limits. While I hated to admit it, being back in Golden had been nice.

I handed over my motel keys, shoved my last suitcase into the truck and slammed it shut.

Once in the car, an overwhelming sense of anxiety rushed over me.

I want that bid!

The thought hit me with such conviction that it surprised me, and I was taken off guard by the deep-rooted desire.

"Okay, chick, you need to chill," I muttered, turning on the ignition and promptly hitting the expressway.

In the distance, the clocktower loomed.

A memory flashed before my eyes, in a brief rebellious stage in our sophomore year, Tori and I had tagged it.

How ridiculous.

I'd never broken the law ever, but Tori had talked me into spray painting Dustin's name on the tower after he stood me up at a football game. We earned him detention for a week.

I laughed.

He never guessed it was me, at least if he did, he'd never mentioned.

Warmth filled my chest, and I realized something; I was smiling. The thought of returning to Golden actually had me smiling, and it kind of freaked me out. I'd been avoiding this place for so long that loathing it felt second nature. But the truth was, now I was back, I was enjoying all the things about this little town that used to drive me insane. Things like knowing my neighbors.

I knew the names of every person up and down Laverne's street. That drove me crazy when I was younger. I hated the idea of everyone in town knowing every little thing about me. Especially when I'd been grieving Steven. I wanted privacy.

In LA, I couldn't tell you the name of a single one of my apartment neighbors. There was big hat guy and purple lipstick girl, but names? No.

Then there was Tori. Having my best friend five minutes down the road again seemed like a faraway fantasy, like part of my past life I couldn't grasp at again.

If I was honest with myself, part of me had always wanted to come home and pick things up where I'd left off.

I pulled up outside Laverne's home; she wasn't there, but she had already given me a key. I carried my suitcases in, ready to unpack. My phone buzzed, and I smiled to see that it was Tori.

"Hello!" I sang, holding the phone with my shoulder as I straightened.

"Hey, girlfriend!" Tori sang right back.

"Aren't you supposed to be working?" I asked.

"I am working," she said. "But I'm the shop's boss, so I take breaks when I want."

Tori had recently taken over her parents' old bait and tackle shop. It went back three generations, and it was passed to Tori when her parents retired early. Tori, though, was an ice-sculpture artist. So, she had renamed the shop: Bait, Beer, & Ice. I hadn't had the opportunity to check out the renovations, but I was going to get a glimpse of it when I meet her for brunch later that day.

"Whatever you say, boss lady," I said, laughing. "What's up?"

"I have good news," she said.

My heart leapt into my throat, and I let out a squeal. "What? Tell me."

"You got the bid!"

"Are you serious? I got the bid?"

"You got the bid," she repeated. "You're going to be renovating the clocktower, museum, and miner statue. You won them over."

"I honestly can't believe it!" I exclaimed, the anxiety I'd had all morning melting away.

"Wow, you sound way more excited than I expected," Tori said. "Glad you're coming around."

"I suppose I've finally admitted to myself that I've missed this place."

"Hazzah!" Tori screamed, and I shook my head.

"Oh, shut up," I said, but I laughed all the same. "I can't believe you couldn't wait another ten minutes to tell me in person. I'm about to head out the door now to meet you at the shop."

"We'll talk more when you get here," she said. "But... well... there's sort of a catch."

I frowned, stopping at the top of the stairs. "What catch?" I asked.

"So... some of the board members were concerned about your experience with small town revivals," she said. "So, um..."

"Spit it out, Tori," I said, making my way down the stairs. I gripped the phone tight to the point I had to force myself to relax.

"They want you to work with one of the architects from Revival," she said.

"What!"

"They have engineers and architects on staff who are going to work as your team," she explained. "We've already discussed this with Revival. The council wants you heading it up, but they want their input and experience."

I shook my head. "Ugh," I said, making my way out the door.

"Look, I got a customer coming in. I'll see you in ten, and we'll talk more."

"Fine," I said, hanging up the phone.

Now I felt flustered. Work with Revival?

Yes, I had gotten the bid, but was the council really going to pay extra to make sure I had a babysitter.

How insulting!

Revival definitely had some experience points on me, sure, but seriously? The council just wanted their cake and eat it. Revival were professionals, but they lacked vision. They were known for pushing big-box stores onto towns once revitalized. I was pretty sure they got a kickback from the stores who wanted to move in, putting the good old-fashioned mom-and-pop stores out of business.

At least if I was in charge, I could keep that from happening. It would be my call, and if the council was giving me the bid, they liked my ideas and concepts better than Revival's. They just lacked faith in me to do it on my own. "Whatever," I scowled as I walked out.

I arrived at a long strip of small-town shops, winding up in front of an older building. It was just as you'd picture an old bait and tackle shop. When I entered, I saw Tori had expanded the bar. Men were gathered around, drinking and telling tales of their fishing experiences. I didn't recognize the server behind the bar, so I bypassed that area and entered the store itself. It was full of more fishing gear than you could find anywhere else.

There had been an addition toward the back of the shop, and it is there I found Tori. The large sign at the end of the hallway read "FREEZER ROOM – EMPLOYEES ONLY," but I entered anyway.

I gasped at the sight of all the ice sculptures. They were small and dainty, but Tori was in the center of the room carving away at an enormous block of ice. I couldn't tell what it was supposed to be, but it looked like it was going to be over seven feet tall. The base looked like legs, so I imagined it was a person of some sort.

"What are you making?" I asked, shivering as I stepped further into the freezer room.

"Uncle Sam," she said, standing upright and spinning around to face me, her chisel in one hand and hammer in the other. "I know, doesn't look like much just yet, but just you wait. It's going to be awesome."

"You're so talented," I said, admiring a beautiful mermaid sculpture, only a few feet tall. "That one is super cute."

"Mermaids! You'd be amazed how many requests I get for mermaids! Uncle Sam here, though, is for the Butter and Egg parade."

"Tori!" I exclaimed. "That's soon. Are you going to have time to finish it?"

"I know. I got a really late start this time around," she admitted. "But thankfully my other projects are finished, so I'm pretty much just going to be working on this one. I've hired some more staff at the shop for the season too, so when I'm here I'm just going to be working on this."

I'd watched her create her incredible pieces before, and I had a good idea on how long these things take. With the festival approaching in a matter of days, I was nervous for her. "Are you sure you have time for brunch today?"

"Are you kidding!" She placed her tools on hooks on the wall. "I've always got time to celebrate with my darling Hope! You got the bid, hon, and we definitely need to celebrate with mimosas. Plus, the cold is starting to get to me now. I need to get warmed up again before I get frostbite!"

"Can you get frostbite in here?" I asked, rubbing my arms on our way out of the room.

"Eh, probably," she said. She'd meant it as a joke but I could tell she now wondered if it was something to be concerned about.

We headed out the front door. Tori waved at the bartender and told her to call if anyone misbehaved, causing the men at the bar to shout and jeer playfully. I shook my head. "You extended that bar in there too, huh?"

"Beer keeps the place open. I'm telling you, that's what pays the bills," Tori said. "Dad should have added to that long ago. Now it's my job. But now let's talk about yours! The committee wants to meet tomorrow with you and Revival's representative. Are you free?"

"Absolutely!" I said. "I'm here for this job, after all. I haven't exactly picked up a bunch of extracurriculars yet, so feel free to assume my calendar is one hundred percent open."

"Excellent," Tori said. "Because I plan on making up for lost time now you're back. In the meantime, we need to get you ready for the next committee meeting. Got to work the budget now we're pulling on both you and Revival."

Great.

They're going to try to talk me down so they could afford Revival as well.

I wasn't about to let that happen. I knew my worth. I just needed to come up with a plan to make sure I stayed on top.

# Chapter Ten

I knew working with Revival was going to be difficult. I'd never partnered with a group like that before, but I felt that I was up for the challenge. I kept wondering who was going to represent them. The committee, according to Tori, wanted me in charge of the whole operation, so I didn't know what they wanted from Revival specifically. My greatest worry was that they would step on my toes.

I pulled up to city hall shortly after lunch for the follow-up meeting. Thankfully, didn't have as much to carry as the last time, just printouts of the design plans I'd presented last time, along with detailed packets on my vision for the town center. They were all neatly tucked into individual files in my shoulder bag.

Stepping out of the car, I spied one of Revival's cars. Their representative had already arrived, it seemed. "This is going to work just fine." I tried to convince myself as I entered the building.

The follow-up meeting was in the same room as before. As I hurried down the hall, I spotted Dustin chatting with Bonnie. "Afternoon," I said.

"Hey, Hope!" Bonnie exclaimed. "Looking forward to what you all have to say today. Really excited to get going on this project."

"Me too. Thanks, Bonnie," I said. I offered Dustin a smile and a nod, and thankfully he returned the gesture.

Probably hasn't heard that I moved in with Aunt Laverne yet, I thought hiding my smile.

The room was set up different this time. The table had been moved to the center of the room; the intention being that we would all sit together as opposed to the committee meeting staring at us across the way like celebrity judges on a reality singing show. Tori was there, chatting with Sharron and Ted while looking over some paperwork I'd left with them after the last meeting.

"Hey, Hope," Tori said, and the others greeted me similarly.

"Afternoon, everyone," I said, looking around until I spotted the Revival rep. It was Sonny, standing aloof in a corner with a coffee mug in hand, enjoying the sunlight coming in from the window. "Sonny, so you're the one I'll be working with?"

Sonny grinned. "Looks that way," he said, tucking a file under his arm and heading over to the table.

I sat down as Dustin and Bonnie reentered the room, finding seats around the table as well. Sonny sat next to me, and alas, the meeting was underway.

"So, Hope, I'm sure you're wondering why Sonny is involved," Dustin began.

"I must admit it's a little unusual," I said.

"We just felt that, given Revival's experience in revitalizing small towns like ours, it would be a good idea for us to form a collaborative contract," he said. "So today, our hope is that we'll be able to work out the details on what that would look like, so we break ground on the clocktower renovations within the next few weeks."

I appreciated Tori's warning from the day before. This was a contract negotiation. The committee wanted to pay what I quoted while keeping Revival on board. By the glimmer in Dustin's eye, I wondered if he was hoping this was going to deter me.

Well, I had news for him.

I knew how to negotiate—and I could do it well.

For the next hour and a half, I listened to Dustin and Bonnie weasel their way around the budget. It was clear what they wanted. I was a freelancer, so they thought they could cut away at my price to make room for Revival's income. Revival, though, were a conglomerate with set prices. Sonny only had so much negotiating power, and he would have to make a phone call to make adjustments. Instead of relenting, I used this to my advantage to get Sonny out of the room.

"Why don't you give your supervisor a call?" I suggested when our negotiations reached a stand still. "See what he says?" I didn't even know if Sonny had a supervisor, but it worked. He stood up, muttered a quick "pardon me for a moment," and left the room.

Dustin grimaced.

Now was time for me to shine. I completely flipped the script and suggested adjustments to Revival's input. The less involvement they had, I explained, the less the price was going to skyrocket. I zeroed in on Bonnie as everyone but her and Dustin wanted me on top. I addressed her concerns as quickly and as professionally as I could while Sonny was not there to counter anything I said, and I managed to win her over.

Dustin writhed in discomfort; I'm pretty sure he knew I had gotten Sonny out of there intentionally.

Sonny returned with "bad news" from his supervisor. He was clearly working some good-guy-bad-guy act to keep as much money in Revival's pocket as possible. But by that time, the committee had scratched a bunch of items off Revival's list of to-dos. Even Dustin seemed swayed, though somewhat begrudgingly, and Sonny looked hard pressed.

"I see. So, you just want us as middle men to get deals on construction materials," he muttered. "Well, we can certainly act as your wholesaler for that sort of thing."

"We still want Revival's input and for you to work closely with Hope moving forward," Dustin said. "But we're going to hand most of the reigns over to Mrs. Wilson."

Oh my gosh, that is killing him to say!

The thought amused me, and I covered my smile with a file, pretending to be highly interested in the document. Tori caught my eye and smirked.

Before I knew it, the contract was drawn up.

We'd been there for two hours, and Sonny looked stressed. I felt bad for him; he was the one guy from Revival who'd shown me kindness, after all. We signed the papers, then Sonny and I stood in the hallway while the committee members remained in the meeting room to discuss notes from the budget meeting.

"How did you manage that?" Sonny asked, looking a mix of irate and impressed. "The guys at Revival are going to have my head when they see how much of this thing has been handed to you."

"They just want your experience," I said. "Not your vision. Don't get me wrong, Revival is impressive. But they're not what Golden needs. I look forward to working with you in the future months, Sonny."

Sonny sighed, but he managed a smile. "And I look forward to working for you, Mrs. Wilson." With those parting words, he sulked away in defeat.

This was going to be my project, and it was written in ink, our signatures at the bottom of the contract. We'd signed not only for the clocktower but for the museum and the statue renovation as well. And I'd persuaded the committee to raise their budget to accommodate Sonny instead of cutting back on what I was going to be getting paid.

This was a major win for me.

The committee meeting dispersed; they all looked very pleased with how things turned out. Tori made a b-line for me, but Dustin beat her to it, and she backed off and rejoined the others.

"A word, Hope?" he asked.

I frowned but nodded. "Sure." We stepped aside as the other committee members left together.

"I'm really impressed, Hope," he admitted, refusing to meet my eyes. "You know your worth. I honestly thought when we started talking about slashing your profit margin you would either cave or bolt."

"I've been doing this for a while now, Dustin," I said. "I know my ideas are good, and I know what I should be getting paid. You know me well enough not to make those assumptions."

I expected him to come back with some sarcastic comment, but instead he laughed at himself. "You know, you're right. I shouldn't have expected anything less from Hope Wilson, now should I have? I suppose I put my foot in my mouth."

I managed to smile. He was being sincere with me; it was so different from the tension we'd had since that grocery store run-in. "Yeah, a little," I said. "Looks like we're going to be working together a good bit over the next year or two. You prepared for that?"

"I'm as prepared as I'll ever be," he said with a sparkle in his eye. "I think we need to call a truce."

"Oh?" I wasn't sure of his motives.

"I'm sorry," he said. I could tell it nearly killed him to say it. I adjusted my footing, standing up straighter, now eager to hear what he had to say. "I have to be honest, I wasn't prepared to see you again. I'm sure it looks like I did everything I could to make sure you weren't the one who got this bid. That's not entirely true, but I must admit part of me didn't want you to get it. I've been terrible toward you. Seeing you, it just reminds me of him, that's all, and I shouldn't have treated you poorly because of it."

That was a complete one-eighty!

"Wow, Dustin..." I stammered. "Thank you for saying that."

"Well, let's put it behind us," he said and then cleared his throat. "I wanted to see how you felt about dinner tonight, to go over some talking points from today's meeting. I have some questions about your bid I want to make sure I'm clear on, and notes from the other committee members I'd like to share with you. My treat, of course."

"Dinner?"

"Yes, dinner," he said. "And I know you're staying with Aunt Laverne now, by the way. Thanks for the heads up on that one."

I chuckled. "She chased me down outside a café and bribed me with butterscotch buttons."

Dustin laughed. "That sounds about right. So, how about I pick you up in..." He checked his watch. "Two hours?"

"That should work for me," I said.

"Great," he said, and we walked toward the exit. "It's a date." I stared at him, and he held up both hands defensively. "I didn't mean it like that."

"I know," I said, but before we could say anything else, Tori bounded toward me.

"Hope! I've got to show you these pictures I took of the ice sculpture. It's really coming along."

I nodded to Dustin before I branched off away from him and followed Tori to her. I got the impression Tori thought she was saving me from Dustin, so I wanted to clear things up.

"Dustin and I are having dinner tonight to go over some talking points from the meeting," I said, and she shot me a perplexed look.

"You two are... having dinner?" she asked.

"To talk about the project," I said. "But yes. I think we're working towards being civil."

Tori studied me before deciding she was satisfied by my response. "Okay, girl, if you think so. I got to go. I got a text during the meeting.

Nolan decided to eat some crayons today at school."

"Oh, gosh!" I exclaimed. "Is he okay?"

"He's fine, but his father's freaking out," she said with a loud sigh. "The joys of parenthood are constant, let me tell you. I've got to get him to the pediatrician. Make sure everything is okay. Techer thinks he ate at least five."

"But why?" I questioned.

"I will never fully understand the way preschooler's think," Tori said. "Like, do the blue ones taste better?"

I stared at her for a moment before realizing she was joking. "Well, you'd better go take care of that. I'll let you know how dinner with Dustin goes."

"You better," she warned before hopping in her car and driving off.

I made my way toward my car, glancing over my shoulder at Dustin. He was watching me from a distance. He smiled, and I smiled back before getting in my car to drive back to Aunt Laverne's.

Apparently, I now had a dinner date to get ready for, and as weird as it seemed, I was actually really looking forward to it.

# Chapter Eleven

Aunt Laverne was absolutely giddy when I told her I was going to dinner with her nephew. She put all her candy making plans aside and hurried up the stairs to the room I was now confidently renting for the long haul. I expected her to fumble, thanks to her injury, but the woman bolted past me and started rummaged through my clothes before I even made it halfway up the stairs.

"What do you think you are doing?" I asked, rounding the top of the stairs and entering the room.

I still hadn't done much to the place. I'd need to pull some of my things out of storage from LA and there was still a few of Wayne's things that hadn't made it downstairs yet. The mess didn't deter Laverne, though. She had my suitcase open on the bed already, pulling out my nicer blouses.

"Ooh, this one is just darling, but I'll have to iron it. You kept in that suitcase too long and now it's just dreadful." She gave the soft pink blouse a shake and held it up in my direction, looking at me past it and then shaking her head. "No, no, you need something with a bit more pop… you've got those lovely undertones in your skin… something… yellow!" She found just what she was looking for and held it out. "Oh, yes, this! This is perfect. And I might have some lovely gold jewelry to go with it."

"You understand this is not a date, right?" I asked as she threw the yellow blouse at me.

"I understand that perfectly, dear," Laverne said, dumping more of my clothes out of the suitcase in search of a skirt. "But I know my Dustin, and he's going to adjust his plans in accordance to how you are dressed."

"I beg your pardon?"

Laverne waved her hand. "I always taught him that a gentleman should show up for an evening with a lady in well-rounded and versatile attire. A nice button-up and prim-pressed jeans would bode well for a relaxed stroll or for something a tad more lavish. If the lady shows up in a dress and heels, he needs to up his game plan, but if she's in a ball cap and t-shirt, he's still dressed in a way that didn't make him look overdressed. It's the lady who decides what's really going on, but the man looks like he knew what he was planning all along."

I blinked, my mind going back to my first date with Steven. Nice blue jeans and a button-up. I had worn a dress and heels, and he had taken me to a really snazzy restaurant. "Was Dustin the only one you gave that bit of advice to?" I asked.

She smirked. "Three plans for a first date, and you tell the lady it's a surprise. Steven was prepped for a fancy dinner, a burger joint and ice cream, or the local batting range. His attire was perfect for all three choices, and he decided where to take you because of what you chose to wear. There were plenty of Dustin's friends who took the wise words of Auntie Laverne, and your sweet Steven was no exception."

It was odd. A warm feeling welled up in me. Hearing someone talk about Steven usually stirred me up and broke me down. But this was a new story I didn't even know. "He really had three different date ideas planned?" I asked, wanting to know more.

"Of course he did!" Aunt Laverne exclaimed. "Steven was as much of a student of mine as Dustin." Her face suddenly fell, and that sick feeling in my gut returned. She exhaled heavily. "I miss him too, you know?"

"I know," I said, still gripping the blouse.

"Now, let's get you taken care of," Laverne said, snapping out of her sadness in an instant and leaving me there alone. She pulled out a black A-line skirt and tossed it at me. I wasn't ready to catch it, but it landed right over my head and shoulder.

"Hey!" I exclaimed, and I laughed, pulling myself from memories of Steven that had started to play in my head like an old film reel. "You know this isn't a date, Laverne!" I warned her, but she wasn't listening to a word I had to say.

She had me in the yellow blouse and black skirt before I knew it, and she picked out a pair of her own black heels and a lovely gold necklace. Soon, I sat in front of her vanity while she styled my hair. I must admit, I was having fun getting dressed up for an evening out.

But then it happened. Just as Laverne finished my hair, my phone buzzed. It was a message from Dustin.

Sorry. Something came up – gonna have to get a rain check

An unexpected wave of disappointment washed over me. Laverne was mortified when I showed her the text from her nephew.

"That rascal!" she exclaimed and pointed at my phone. "You text him and tell him his aunt is furious with him for standing up such a sweet doll!"

I laughed and put on a smile, but truthfully, the last-minute cancelation hurt. "It's fine, Aunt Laverne. Like I told you, it was just a business meeting."

Aunt Laverne gave me knowing look that I didn't care for. I could practically hear her saying you and I both know that's not true, Hope.

I looked at my reflection, and I felt better than I had in a while. I looked good; Laverne had done a great job. "But you know what?" I said, standing,

"I'd hate to waste all the time you spent fancying me up. I just might take myself out to dinner tonight."

"That's my girl!" Laverne exclaimed. "Go paint the town red! Knock 'em all dead."

I laughed. "Care to join me?"

Laverne waved her hand. "Oh, certainly not! I have far too many candies to make tonight."

"Are you sure?"

"I'm sure, dear. Spoil yourself. Order a steak or something," Laverne said, and I smiled appreciatively at her.

I was painfully betrayed by Dustin's last-minute cancelation. Was he lying about something coming up?

He chickened out and didn't want to meet me, I decided.

I snagged my purse and left, trying not to look like I was storming off. I didn't want Laverne giving Dustin a hard time because then he'd know I was upset. I didn't want him to know canceling dinner plans had gotten to me. I strutted off confidently so Laverne would at least think I was looking forward to an evening by myself.

But I wasn't.

Laverne's high heels were a size too small and my toes were squashed as I walked downtown. I quickly regretted deciding to walk. These things were going to give me blisters, so I hurried to the closest eatery I could find. There was a little tavern five minutes from Laverne's that had been there as long as I could remember.

It was a bar and grill type place. I was over-dressed, but I knew I could get a good steak there, and Laverne had put that in my head. I stepped into the bar and to my horror, I knew every single person currently in the room.

Shoot!

It was as though every person I went to high school with was out tonight. People I knew from book club or local shop owners I used to greet daily stared at me, and I froze. The hostess, a woman I knew from my, greeted me at the door. "Miss Hope!" she said perkily. "Wow, long time no see!"

"Hi, Melissa," I said. Every part of me wanted to bolt out that door and suck up the blisters already forming.

"Table for one or two?" she asked me.

A few people at the bar turned their heads, then spun back, whispering to one another. "Is that Hope Wilson?"

"Nah, she moved to LA or something."

"No, I really think that's her…"

I wanted to die, but I wasn't about to run back to Laverne's. If I did, Dustin would win, and I wouldn't let him completely ruin my evening. I had gotten the bid. That meant I was going to be here for a long while, and I needed to confront this.

Taking a deep breath, I said, "Table for one. Thank you, Melissa." She led me to a table in the center of the tavern.

The couple at the next table grinned at me. "Hope, when did you get back in town?"

"Hey, Phil. Hey, Angela," I said. "I'm actually here for work. I've been commissioned to head up the restoration of the clocktower."

"It's about time!" Angela said, nudging her husband. I had been in book club with Angela for years before Steven's passing. "The clocktower stopped working a few weeks ago. The place is looking rough. I'm so glad they got a Golden girl to work on that! I've heard you've been doing really well in the architectural world."

I thanked her, and the couple went back to their own conversation, but they were far from the last interaction I would have that evening. The server, Tommy, was thrilled to see me. I went to high school with his mother; he was the uh-oh baby born to an unwedded teenager. Tori and I had been among those who had helped her out in those early days of small-town ridicule, a fact his mother had never let him forget. He even called us aunts when he was small.

"I can't wait to tell Mom you're back in town," he said, all smiles. "She'd love to get together."

Anxiety welled in my stomach. I really didn't want to see my old friends. I knew they stir up memories of Steven, but I had to get over that if I was going to hang around. "Absolutely. I'd love to see Kristin."

He took my order and hurried off to get me a water. People drifted from the bar to say hello, and I forced myself to talk with them. It became less painful the more people I spoke to. They were all happy to see me, and I felt loved and missed by my hometown. It felt good, even if it did bring up old memories of Steven.

I thanked Tommy as brought steak and refilled my water. Now I that I was eating, people seemed less inclined to approach me, and I was glad. I needed break from it to link old wounds.

The food was as good as I remembered it being. Steven and I had always liked this tavern. You could get high-quality food for a bar-and-grill price. Just as I settled into the familiarity, the universe tested my limits again.

"No way! Mrs. Wilson! Mrs. Wilson!"

I glanced up to see who had just entered the tavern, and my stomach dropped. It was a family of three: a mother, a father, and a young son in a wheelchair. It was the teenager who had shouted at me from across the way. His name was Peter Lentz, and he was with Steven the day he died.

# Chapter Twelve

"Peter," I said, my voice so raspy it hardly sounded like me at all. I took a sip of my water as the young man wheeled himself to my table. He had a small, sleek wheelchair that allowed him to easily whip around the other tables, so he reached me in an instance.

"Mrs. Wilson! Wow, I heard you were back in town, but I didn't think I'd run into you."

My stomach twisted and a wave of guilt to rushed over me.

Peter had only been fourteen years old when it happened; I hadn't seen him since the funeral, and that was nearly five years ago. I'd spoken to him a couple of times on the phone and had him a card for his birthday, but I kept him at arm's length. Steven had saved Peter – that's what the coroner had told me.

He had drowned himself in the process.

My husband had worked with disabled children as a volunteer sports therapist for years. He and Peter were exceptionally close, and Steven had taken him out to kayak in the nearby river. The floods made the rapids more dangerous than Steven had anticipated. The same river he had kayaked up and down with children like Peter a thousand times before killed him.

The change in Peter was dramatic. It was the same feeling I got when looking at pictures of Tori's son. Peter was no longer that scared fourteen-year-old I'd sat with in the hospital, trying to reassure him that it Steven's death hadn't been his fault. Peter's kayak had capsized, and Steven had sacrificed himself to get the boy back into the kayak safely. It was hard to believe this young man staring back at me was that same boy who had been the first to mourn with me that day.

"Look at you," I managed to say after another swallow. "Gosh, Peter, I almost didn't recognize you."

He positively glowed. "Yeah, it's been a while," he said. "What brings you back to Golden?"

"Work," I said. "I have been asked to work on the clocktower's restoration. What have you been up to?"

"I'm in college now," he said excitedly, and the thought stunted me. He had to be nineteen now, but I still pictured him as a high-school freshman. "I'm studying investigative journalism."

"That's really awesome, Peter."

Peter's parents joined us. "Peter, she's having dinner," his mother warned, but the woman paused and smiled at me. "Hope, it's really nice seeing you back in town."

I smiled. "It's good to be back."

"We'll let you eat," his father said. "Sorry for the interruption."

"It's really no interruption at all." I watched Peter zip back through the tavern to a corner booth. I realized how much I've missed that kid. I've probably thought about him more than anyone else. He felt so guilty for not being able to help Steven; I could have been here for him.

I should have been.

But seeing him smiling like that? He was okay, and I knew that now. My airways seemed to open up, and I released tension in my shoulders.

I finished my dinner, but before I could consider the possibility of dessert, someone else disturbed me. Belinda Johnson, she jumped of her seat at the bar and sauntered in my direction. She had a reputation for liking a drink.

"Getting started early, Belinda?" I teased as she double stepped to avoid tripping on the way to my table.

Belinda plopped down in the chair next to me without asking if she could join. She smiled that big toothy smile of hers. "Now don't you go reprimanding me, Miss Hope Wilson," she said. "Naughty girl. You and I are going to go for drinks so you can tell me all about your misadventures, Miss big time Hollywood."

I laughed. Belinda was from LA herself. Her family had moved to Golden halfway through her senior year of high school, which had been rough on her. She had created a grand personality for herself playing up the LA background for attention. It continued long after we graduated, and it came to be expected by her peers. She was popular back then, and she still was now.

She passed the bar exam a few years back and was a local lawyer who made her money in a small claims court, helping people to sue for ridiculous trespasses.

"You would know more about LA misadventures than I would, Belinda," I said, and she laughed loudly.

"Oh, come on, you know I haven't been to LA in ages," she said. "But I would love to swap tales with you sometime. How long have you been back in Golden?"

"Just a few weeks," I said. "At least nearby. I've only just moved into a place in town. Been staying at the motel for while."

Belinda threw back the drink in her hand, finishing it off in a single gulp. I raised my brow. It really was early to be throwing back her drinks like that, even by Belinda's standards.

"Everything… all right?"

"Fine, hon," she said, waving the bartender over.

A man put his hand out to stop the bartender coming over, passing him some cash and shaking his head before coming our way. "Babe, I think you're bothering this woman," the man said, looking irritable.

"Oh, shut up, Mark," Belinda said. "Did you just tell the bartender to cut me off?"

"I think we should get you home," he said.

"You're acting like I'm wasted," Belinda hissed. "And she isn't this woman. This is Hope. We went to high school together."

The man went red in the face. "Oh," he said. "I'm sorry… I thought…"

"That I was so far gone I was harassing a stranger trying to enjoy her meal?" Belinda questioned. "Lighten up." She turned her attention back to me. "This goofball is Mark. We've been dating for a while, but I'm probably going to ditch him soon."

"Babe…" he whined like a beaten puppy dog, and I bit my lip to keep from snickering. He caught me stifling my laugh and tightened his shoulders. "Mark Sanders," he said. "Nice to meet you."

"You too," I said. "You sure you can handle this one, Mark?" I asked, giving him a wink.

He laughed. "Doing my best."

"You're terrible," Belinda said to me, but she laughed all the same. "Well, clearly, my ride is ready to go. I'll call you soon, okay, Hope? I really would love to catch up sometime."

"I look forward to it," I said, and I watched Belinda grab Mark's arm aggressively before he escorted her out the door.

The server brought my tab and as I was signing my check, Peter broke away from his parents. "I saw you talking to Belinda," he said. "Did she say anything about Wayne Maloney?"

I dropped the pen in surprise at the dead man's name. "Why would Belinda say anything about Wayne Maloney? Better question – how do you know Wayne Maloney?"

Peter grinned. "Oh, I don't know him, but I did manage to find out he was the dead guy in the clocktower."

"And just how did you find that out?"

"I've got my sources," Peter said. "I told you I'm doing investigative journalism, remember?"

"You planning on writing an article on this or something?" I asked.

"Maybe," he said. "So, what did Belinda have to say about Wayne? She told me to f-off when I asked about the bar fight."

"What bar fight?"

Peter frowned. "Darn, I was hoping she was tipsy enough to have said something to you."

"Peter!" I said.

"Her boyfriend and Maloney got into a fight in this tavern the night before you found his body," Peter said. "Supposedly Wayne was getting a little handsy with Belinda, and Mark wailed on the guy. I wasn't here, so it's all he-said-she-said, but I've talked to a few witnesses who were here when Wayne got thrown out of the bar."

Pride welled up inside me. Peter wasn't my son, but he had come pretty close to it back in the day. Steven invested so much time and energy into Peter, he would have been so proud to hear he was in college and working toward an exciting career. There was a look of passion about him that was simply beautiful on his young face.

"I'm impressed," I said, and this made him light up even more. "So... what else do you know about Maloney?"

"Not so fast," he said, pointing a finger in my direction. "I told you something I knew. Now you tell me about finding Maloney."

I frowned. "I don't know if I should. The police haven't even released his name yet and..." I paused. "Wait. You didn't know for sure it was Maloney, did you? You tricked me into confirming that for you!" The look he gave me was the most devious thing I had ever seen. He had pulled a reporter's trick on me, and I hadn't seen it coming. "Rotten little scoundrel," I said, but I smiled. "Okay, fine. What do you want to know?"

"What was the crime scene like? And can you tell me the names of the responding officers?" he asked.

I probably shouldn't have, but I gave him what he was looking for, along with a warning not to get himself into trouble. He wrote it down in a small notepad and when he was done scribbling, I gave him a nudge. "Now what else do you know, Mr. Detective?"

"You know Charlie Olson?" he asked.

"Yeah, he owns half the gold mines around here," I said.

"So, I went down to the courthouse and did a search on Wayne. He had an open case against Charlie Olson and George Peterson."

A knot formed in my throat.

George Peterson? As in, Dustin's father?

"For what?" I asked.

"Wayne worked in Lyons' gold mine, the one about ten miles from here. He got hurt on the job, and he was preparing a lawsuit over the working conditions in the mines," Peter explained. "And if it had gone through, Olson would be liable for not just Wayne's injuries. A whole plethora of employees were backing Wayne and potentially doing a class action lawsuit. Olson might have wanted to keep Wayne from following through."

"What about Mr. Peterson?" I asked.

"Looking at what the court had, it seemed the lawsuit was leaning more toward E-Goldrush and less toward the individual owner of the mine, but I'm not willing to say it didn't touch a nerve with Peterson," Peter explained. "It was Olson who had the real crisis on his hands, and that's magically gone away now Wayne's out of the picture. I tried asking Belinda about that too, but it ticked her even more."

"Why would you ask Belinda about the lawsuit?"

"Who do you think Maloney's lawyer was? Only Belinda is dumb enough to take on Olson. Every other lawyer Maloney went too brushed him off. Belinda's always happy to draw attention to herself, and taking on a case against Charlie Olson..."

"That explains why her boyfriend got into it with Wayne," I said. "She was probably spending a lot of time with Maloney, and he started to get jealous."

"Maybe, but the rumor is that Maloney was being pretty flirty with her," Peter said. "Who knows whether Belinda and Maloney were here for professional reasons or for personal ones. Anyways, there's a lot more to this than the police are willing to dig up. Olson was getting sued by Maloney. That much I know for sure, and let's be honest, Charlie Olson has a reputation for being less than civil when people threaten his money."

"Peter, if you're right about this, you could get yourself in the middle of something dangerous."

He held up both hands defensively. "All right, I'll ease up," he said. "But either way, thanks for the confirmation, Mrs. Wilson. It really is good to see you. I've missed you."

I smile at him. "I've missed you too, you stubborn little brat." I reached over and rubbed the top of his head like I had seen Steven do a thousand times. I did it out of instinct, not really thinking about it, but I could see it jarred him. After the look of surprise faded, a sad looking smile replaced it.

He rejoined his parents at their booth, and I could hear his mother scolding him for bothering me so much, but honestly it really wasn't a bother. I wasn't sure what I would feel when I had run into Peter, but now I had, and I was honestly happy. Seeing Peter reminded me of Steven, but it didn't break my heart like I'd feared it would.

It warmed it.

# Chapter Thirteen

By the time I left the tavern, the sun was setting on Golden. I never minded walking the streets at night here. It was peaceful, so different to LA where the nightlife never ended. In Golden, it seemed like the only ones out this late were a few local tavern goers and a handful of troublesome teens. There was always the occasional night jogger, too, one of whom I nodded at as we crossed paths on the sidewalk.

I was quickly reminded of the pain in my feet from earlier that evening as I crossed the street toward home.

Note to self: never borrow Aunt Laverne's shoes again.

The shoes were tearing the skin off the back of my right foot. I finally gave up and took them off, electing to go barefoot.

"Yikes," I said, leaning against the crosswalk pole and lifting my foot to examine the damage.

It was just dark enough that I worried I'd step on glass or something sharp, but I also didn't want to put the shoes on again. I pulled out my cellphone and opened my flashlight app, shining the light in front of me as I walked.

The streetlights ended after the shops, and it was just me and my phone light leading the way back to Aunt Laverne's.

And then the inevitable happened.

I stepped on something.

"Ouch!" I yelped, stepping back in annoyance. An acorn had pierced the ball of my foot, sending a painful jolt up my leg. When I stepped back, I pivoted, and my light caught the outline of a hooded person a few yards back, peering around a fence.

"Um..." I muttered nervously as the figure darted around the corner, intentionally avoiding my gaze. "Is someone there?" I called out.

If I was in LA, I'd have already had my pepper spray ready. But this wasn't LA; I hadn't even bothered bringing my pepper spray to Golden. My heart raced, aware no one else was around. "I saw you!" I shouted into the darkness.

"You and that crippled kid need to back the hell off," a deep voice grumbled. "Or someone else is going to get hurt."

I instinctually dropped my shoes and took a defensive stance. "Who's there!" I shouted again and inched closer to the fence. My breathing quickened as I reached the corner. I spun around, light up and ready.

But whoever it was had disappeared.

I felt a rush of panic. I had no idea where he had gone.

Was he going to sneak up on me?

Jump me?

The adrenaline rush hit me hard, and I bolted. I ran the rest of the way to Aunt Laverne's house, stepping on plenty more acorns along the way but not caring one bit.

I rushed through the front door and screamed, "Aunt Laverne? Are you home?"

The last person I expected to see was Dustin, but there he was. He must have sensed the panic in my tone because he raced into the kitchen from the dining room.

He looked me up and down. "Where are your shoes?"

I cussed under my breath, realizing I had abandoned Laverne's shoes in my panic. "Someone was following me," I said, still breathless from my sprint. "What... what are you doing here?"

I put my hands on my knees. I felt stupid standing there so completely out of breath. I glanced up from my bent over position. Dustin looked distraught. "Are you okay?" I asked.

"It's Aunt Laverne," he said. "She called me because the sheriff was banging on her door, but by the time I got here she was gone. They've got her at the station."

"For what?" I asked.

"I'm not sure. I just know she was upset," he said, fumbling over his words.

"Let me get some shoes," I said, hurrying past him. "I'll go with you to the station."

I couldn't imagine what the sheriff wanted with Aunt Laverne. Knowing her, it was some mild infraction that escalated thanks to her attitude. Maybe James was on a power trip. I was still annoyed with Dustin for bailing on me, but we brushed that aside for Aunt Laverne.

He offered to drive and before we even got out of the driveway, he asked me again about my lack of shoes. "I told you, someone was following me. And they warned me to mind my own business. It was scary, and they even brought Peter into it."

"Who?"

"You know of him," I said. "Peter Lentz."

Dustin tensed, and I knew he was thinking about Steven. Since arriving in Golden, one thing I realized was just how much everyone else missed him too. Dustin especially.

"So... someone's threatening you and the kid?" Dustin asked.

"It felt threatening enough for me to ditch your aunt's shoes and bolt," I said.

Dustin did not look amused. "Well, you should report it since we're going to the station anyways," he said, and I agreed.

Once we arrived at the station, we made our way inside, scanning the area. "Aunt Laverne!" Dustin exclaimed the moment he saw her on the bench out front.

Sheriff James Groth was standing near her, and he wisely took a step away as Dustin approached.

"What happened?" I asked.

Laverne rolled her eyes and pointed an accusatory finger at James. "That boy dragged me from my house to come be interrogated."

"Now hold on just a second, Laverne," James stammered. "You came willingly. You don't need to make it sound like I forced you."

"You were rather insistent," Laverne said, crossing her arms and leaning back into the bench.

"What's this about, James?" Dustin snapped.

"We got an anonymous call saying Laverne was responsible for what happened at the clocktower," James said, and both Dustin and I erupted at once.

"That's crazy!" Dustin shouting.

"What's the matter with you, James?" I yelled.

Laverne waved her accusatory finger once more. "See, now, that's what I said. But don't worry, James here has already confirmed my alibi—evidently, I needed one. I was making candies with my friend Blanche. Blanche told him off too."

James scoffed at us. "I'm just doing my job. I wasn't arresting you, Laverne. I just needed to question you about the anonymous tip we received."

"Why would someone call with that nonsense?" Laverne asked. "Just because I kicked that man out of my house. He wasn't paying me. Let me tell you how much that man owed me. He owed me—"

"Aunt Laverne," Dustin said quickly. "Maybe don't start shouting your possible motives at the sheriff?"

Laverne huffed, but didn't say anything more.

"James, earlier tonight, someone tried following me home. I didn't see a face, but they threatened me. I'm guessing whoever it was is the same person who called you about Laverne," I said.

"Someone threatened you?" Laverne asked me, sitting upright and looking like she was ready to start a fight.

"I'm fine," I said.

"You say this person threatened you?" James questioned. "What did they say?"

"They said 'you and that crippled kid need to back the hell off, or someone else is going to get hurt'. And I tried to shine my phone's flashlight on them to see who it was, but they disappeared," I explained. "It freaked me out so much I ran all the way back to Laverne's house completely barefoot… oh, your shoes! Laverne, I'm so sorry, I ditched your shoes on the sidewalk."

"Don't worry about that, dear. I'm just glad you're all right," she said.

"Look, I think this evening has gotten completely blown out of proportion," James said. "We ruled Wayne's death an accident. I just needed to follow up with that anonymous call we received. I'm sorry we got you upset, Laverne, but—"

"No, no, James, it's fine," Laverne said, standing up. "Just maybe next time try calling me before banging on my door like that."

I was annoyed that James didn't seem to be taking my report seriously, but since he was releasing Laverne, I decided to drop it for the time being. Being accused of murder, even if it was an anonymous call, was serious, and we were all lucky that Laverne wasn't being held overnight.

"Hey, Dustin," I said as the three of us left the station. "If you don't mind taking Main Street back, we can look and see if we can get your aunt's shoes back. Maybe they're still where I dropped them?"

Dustin agreed, and I loaded into the back seat while Laverne sat beside her nephew up front. We arrived at the fence where I had stepped on that stupid acorn, and the road was deserted. Dustin and his aunt stayed in the car while I jumped out to look for the shoes. I spotted them right where I had left them, relieved I hadn't cost Aunt Laverne a nice pair of shoes.

I picked them up and started walking back to the car with my phone's flashlight lighting my path. As I did so, I saw something shimmer in the grass near the fence. I bent over and picked up what appeared to be a man's ring.

"What's this?" I asked, holding it to the light.

Dustin poked his head out the window, a scowl on his face. "What are you doing out there?" he snapped. "Quit fooling around and get in the car so I can get my aunt home already. I don't have all night."

I shot him a dirty look, and he quickly rolled up his window as if he thought I'd chunk the shoes at him. I pocketed the ring and climbed into the back seat of the car, catching Dustin's eye in the rearview mirror.

He seemed apologetic for snapping at me.

While we drove back to Laverne's, I pulled the ring out of my pocket and shined my phone's light on it. It was a class ring, and I recognized the school's logo immediately. It was the University of California, Los Angeles. I'd passed that place a thousand times on my way to jobs in and around the city.

"How did this get here…" I pondered, but I suspected I already knew.

Whoever was following me had dropped it. It must have slipped off his finger when he turned to run.

I nodded to myself; I had found a clue that was going to help me figure out who really killed Wayne Maloney.

I put the ring back into my pocket. I knew that this little ring was going to mean big things. The police were still calling the incident an accident, even after someone tried accusing Laverne of killing Wayne.

I wasn't buying it at all.

There was something dirty happening in my home town, and I was determined to figure out what.

# Chapter Fourteen

"Come on..." I said, checking my phone for the fourth time that morning. I'd been calling Sonny since I had gotten up, and he failed time and time again to answer.

It was getting frustrating.

In between making unanswered calls, I dressed, then made my way downstairs in a tantrum-like strut.

Aunt Laverne was in the kitchen rolling candies, and she called to me from her seat.

"You know this is an old house, Hope. Better not go stomping down the stairs, or you'll wind up snapping a board!"

Embarrassed that I had gotten caught throwing a fit, I slowly slid my way into the kitchen.

"Sorry, Laverne," I said. "I'm having a hard time getting hold of my connect at Revival. We're supposed to meet today to discuss breaking ground on the renovation project, but he's not answering any of my calls or texts. I'm thinking about just calling his firm."

"Do that, and get his butt in trouble for slacking off," Aunt Laverne teased.

I sat down with her and started wrapping the candies, plopping only one in my mouth as I did so.

Yay will power!

"Festival's coming up quick, isn't it?" I asked.

Aunt Laverne nodded. "You're telling me. I still have another thousand or so pieces to make and wrap."

"How are you holding up after last night's misadventures?" I asked.

Laverne threw her head back in laughter. "Oh, I know I'm getting on up, honey, but it takes more than an annoying kid playing cop to rattle me."

"Come on, now, don't be giving James that hard a time. He does a good job from what I've heard," I said. "And something tells me, you might have exaggerated him banging on your door when you spoke to Dustin on the phone. Am I right?"

Aunt Laverne didn't answer me with words; she simply grinned and held a finger up to her lips. I shook my head.

"You're terrible getting Dustin worked up like that. But I agree that taking you to the station to answer a few questions seemed a bit much."

"I'm more concerned about you, dear," Aunt Laverne said. "Someone really followed you home from the tavern like that and threatened you? You should give Peter's parents a call—you said the man who followed you mentioned him too, right?"

"Yeah, that was pretty upsetting," I said. I wondered whether it would have stirred me up so much if the stranger had left Peter out of it.

"Speaking of phone calls," Aunt Laverne said, leaning back in her seat to stretch her back. "Have you called the Wilson's since you got back in town?"

I felt instantly sickened with guilt for not having reached out to my in-laws. I had been trying to avoid everyone. Seeing Peter the day before had been hurtful enough. My own folks had retired to Florida not long before Steven died, so in those last few years of my marriage to Steven, I had gotten exceptionally close to his parents. And then I had just run, hardly speaking to them at all in the past five years. There was a lot of guilt from that too.

"I know I should have done so already," I said. "I plan on speaking to them soon."

Aunt Laverne nodded before going back to her candies. I checked my phone repeatedly, managing to roll a half dozen candies in between each glance.

"Okay, I think I'm just going to head to the clocktower," I said after sitting with her for over an hour, waiting on Sonny. "Going to go be productive even if Sonny is flaking. Get some measurements taken care of."

"Atta girl," Aunt Laverne said. "I'll be here. And watch out for yourself."

I nodded. "I will."

I made my way out the door and drove to the clocktower, checking my phone at every stop sign along the way.

"Idiot," I muttered. I had actually liked Sonny. At first, I was annoyed the committee wanted me to work with Revival, but Sonny had had a pleasant disposition. I had started to look forward to working with him, but that feeling was quickly fading.

As the clocktower came into view, I saw an ambulance and two police cruisers parked out front. "Oh, no," I groaned. "What now?"

I parked my car and hurried out, walking up to the clocktower. I spied Officer Barney Stent among the small group of policemen and since we had met once before, I targeted him. "Officer Stent," I said loudly as I approached.

He waved off the other officers and met me halfway down the walkway. "What are you doing here?" he asked, sounding irritated. "You and I need to stop meeting at crime scenes."

"I'm the architect they've hired to work on the tower," I said. "I'm supposed to be here. What's going on?" Officer Stent glared at me, and I didn't care for it. I crossed my arms and glared right back. "I'm sorry, did I do something to offend you?"

"Does the name Sonny Bono mean anything to you?" Officer Stent asked.

"Yeah, he writes good music," I snapped because Stent was leaning really close in, like he was accusing me of something.

"Mrs. Wilson, I suggest you drop the attitude," he said. "Sonny Bono – do you know him?"

"Yeah," I said, uncrossing my arms and attempting to wipe the look off my face. "I've been calling him all morning."

"And why were you calling him?" Officer Stent asked.

I felt flustered, but I knew annoyance would get me nowhere, so I bit my tongue before I said something obnoxious. "The budget committee wanted his agency, Revival, to work with me on the project."

"You were competing with Revival for the bid, right?" he asked.

"Yeah, but—"

Next thing I knew, he was whipping out handcuffs. "Whoa," I said, taking a step back. "What do you think you're doing?"

"Taking you in for questioning, that's what," he said, reaching out to grab my arm.

"Back off! Are you arresting me?" I questioned.

"Ease up, Stent!" a voice boomed a short distance off. I glanced up and saw Sherriff James hurrying over.

"She's got motive, Sheriff," Officer Stent said. My head spun from confusion.

"She's also got an alibi," James said.

"Who?"

"Me, dumby," he said. "She was at the station last night and went home with Dustin and Laverne."

"But we don't know how long—" Officer Stent started to argue, but James cut him off and told him to find a way to make himself useful.

The tension in my chest loosened. I took a breath once Officer Stent was gone and looked at James, still morbidly confused. "James, what happened?"

"The engineer the committee hired to come in and do a follow-up inspection showed up this morning. He opened up a back room and found Sonny Bono passed out and hardly breathing," Sheriff James explained and then nodded towards the ambulance that was pulling out of the parking lot with it's lights on, already blaring its siren. "It's not looking good for Sonny."

"Oh my gosh!"

"We're still trying to figure out what happened," James said, watching the ambulance speed off. "But he was locked inside that back room, couldn't get out. We need to figure out why he started suffocating."

"And… Barney Fife over there thinks I did something to him?" I asked.

Sheriff James snorted. "Barney Fife… that's good. I'm going to remember that," he said. "Yeah, Barney thinks somebody turned the lock around and locked Sonny in. He looks like he had some sort of reaction."

"Poor Sonny," I said. "So, Barney thinks someone locked him in the room while he was having a reaction?"

"It looks that way," James said. "But I'm not jumping to conclusions. Maybe Sonny got himself locked back there somehow. But that doesn't explain why he was passed out and turning blue in the face."

I wasn't going to get any work done at the clocktower while the police were rummaging around. I headed to the hospital instead, assuming no one at Revival knew about Sonny's accident

On the way, I used my Bluetooth to call the number on the back of the business card I'd snagged during the first committee meeting. Adam Douglas answered the call, apparently thinking I was someone from the committee because he started sweet-talking me immediately. "Decided to hire us, did you?" he sang.

"Hey, big shot, it's Hope Wilson," I said. "And, no, they hired me, remember?"

Adam didn't find this at all funny. "What do you want?" he snapped.

Ooh, I hurt his feelings, I thought with amusement.

"I'm en route to the hospital. Sonny was found in the clocktower this morning passed out and having a hard time breathing. I thought I should let someone at Revival know what's going on."

"Geez," Adam said in surprise. "Is he all right?"

"I'm not sure," I said. "I'm heading to the hospital now. I'm not too far behind the ambulance."

"I'm going to head out that way too," Adam said. "Thanks for letting us know, Mrs. Wilson."

"Of course," I said.

"I'm pretty far out… I was on my way to the airport," Adam said. "But I'm turning around. Would you mind calling me if you hear anything? I'd better call his sister…"

"Of course," I said, and we hung up the phone.

I pulled up to the hospital a few short minutes later and texted Adam to let him know I'd arrived.

I hurried into the emergency room and asked about Sonny. I was told to sit in the waiting room until the nurse could get an update on his condition. I was there for about fifteen minutes, fiddling with my phone, before a nurse finally approached me.

"You were the one asking about Sonny Bono?' she asked.

"That's right." I jumped up from my seat. "How is he doing? Is he okay?"

"I'm so sorry," she said, her eyes filled with sympathy. "But Sonny didn't survive the ride to the hospital."

My stomach dropped. "What?" I questioned. "What do you mean?"

"He died on the ambulance ride over," she said. "I'm so very sorry. Were you two close?"

"No, I barely knew him," I said. "We just met a few days ago, but we were going to be working on a project together. I need to make some phone calls."

"Of course," the nurse said.

I stepped out into the hallway, flustered. I called Adam Douglas first, and when he answered I almost didn't have the heart to tell him his coworker was dead. "I'm so sorry, Adam," I said. "But Sonny died on the ambulance ride to the hospital."

"What!" Adam shrieked. "What do you mean he's dead? He died? What happened?"

"I'm not really sure," I said. "I'm going to see if I can speak to the doctor. Are you still coming?"

"Yes, I'm coming," Adam said. "He's… he's really gone?"

"Yes," I said. "I haven't seen him, but that's what the ER nurse told me. I'll be here when you get here."

"Thank you," Adam said breathlessly. "Goodness… I don't know how I'm going to tell Cher this."

"You and Sonny were close?" I asked.

"I'd say so," Adam said. "I got to go. I need to make some phone calls."

I informed the nurse I wanted to speak to someone about what happened to Sonny. She asked me to sit in the waiting room again. I sat down, too distraught to even scroll through social media. Several minutes ticked by before a doctor approached me. I stood up, feeling lightheaded.

"I'm Dr. Roman," the man said, and I shook his hand. "You were asking about Sonny Bono?"

"Yes," I said. "Please, what happened? Can you tell me anything?"

He hesitated. "Are you next of kin?"

Now it was my turn to hesitate, but I found my voice quickly. "Yes, he was my fiancé," I fibbed.

The Dr. barely blinked, the onlynodded and turned on his heels, leading me out of ER and to the back hall. "Come with me."

# Chapter Fifteen

Dr. Roman led me to the back hallway where Sonny's body was laid out on a gurney. Two nurses pushed the gurney toward a back room, and I walked alongside Dr. Roman, following them.

"I can't believe he's gone," I mumbled. That was true enough. I really couldn't believe it. We entered the room, evidently the hospital's morgue. "We're not sure what killed him," Dr. Roman said flatly.

"You mean you don't know?" I asked.

"He only just got here, Miss," he said. "But from the looks of it, I would say he suffocated."

"Suffocated?" I asked.

"Do you happen to know if Mr. Bono was asthmatic?" he asked. "His oxygen levels were very low according to the paramedics."

I stared at the gurney. Sonny was covered by a sheet. It was hard to imagine him lifeless. "I don't know," I said.

Dr. Roman eyed me suspiciously.

"He never told me," I clarified. "Do you mind if I see him?"

Dr. Roman nodded and stepped toward the gurney. The nurses stepped around us, one of them uttering "We're sorry for your loss," on the way out.

I felt strange being the first person at Sonny's side; and lying about our relationship. We didn't have much of a history, or any history, really.

My stomach tightened as Dr. Roman pulled back the cloth, revealing Sonny's face. His lips were tinted purple, but otherwise he looked like he was sleeping. It was now I realized what a handsome guy he was, a fact I'd looked past because of how annoyed I'd been at Revival's presence. All I really knew about him was that his parents had a sick sense of humor for naming him and his sister after one of the most famous singing couples in American history.

Were his parents still around?

Adam told me he was going to call his sister and that made me discombobulated, feeling sympathy for a woman I'd never met. Was she going to be dealing with this alone?

"You don't have to stay here," Dr. Roman said. "I understand how uncomfortable this can be."

"I want to stay," I said. "I don't want him to be alone."

Dr. Roman said, "The coroner has ordered an autopsy to be conducted. Once the forensic pathologist gets in, you're going to have to leave."

"I understand," I said.

"I'll come back and let you know when he arrives," Dr. Roman said, and he left me alone with Sonny.

I stared at the man on the gurney. I couldn't believe how sad I felt for this stranger. I felt claustrophobic imagining Sonny alone in that room, suffocating. I couldn't imagine what had caused it. After a moment of being in the room with him alone, I grew braver and stepped closer to examine him myself.

I pulled the sheet back, deciding to check his pockets for some sort of clue. I found an inhaler. "So, asthma is what did you in, eh, Sonny?" I asked, pressing the inhaler to confirm it was empty. I returned it to his pocket. The only other thing on him was his car keys. I touched the top of his hand apologetically.

"This sucks... what a way to go out..." My eyes fell to his hand. His knuckles felt rough and drew my attention.

"Ouch," I muttered when I saw his hands. His knuckles had dried blood on them. He must have tried to escape the room with gusto, enough to cause damage to his hands. There were even splinters. I could imagine it, the panic he must have felt when he realized he was locked in. Then he had overexerted himself trying to break free. If he was asthmatic and lost his breath like that, then discovered his inhaler wasn't going to help him regain his breath... That would have led him to panic even more.

No longer able to look at him I covered him up. Now that I had pieced together what had likely been his final moments, I turned my attention to the real question; how did he get locked in that room in the first place?

My phone rang. It was Adam. I answered promptly. "You here?"

"Yes, where are you?" he asked.

"I'm in the back with Sonny. They know you're coming. Just let them know at the desk," I said, and he hung up.

Adam appeared in the doorway, having been escorted by a nurse. The man looked terrible. I'd had this picture in my head of the Revival group as a bunch of uptight guys in suits, but they were real people; flesh and blood with hearts and feelings.

Adam hurried over, and I pulled back the sheet for him to see for himself. He had clearly been fighting the urge to cry, and he didn't have any resistance left.

Poor man, he cried over his friend and I stood awkwardly by until Dr. Roman reappeared, telling us to leave because the forensic pathologist had arrived.

I walked with Adam silently back to the ER's waiting room and went and got him a bottle of water from a nearby vending machine. He wiped his face, forcing himself to recollect his bearings now that we were out in public.

"Thank you," he said, taking the water and drinking it.

"I didn't realize you Revival guys were so, I don't know…"

"We're a big company, Miss Hope, but that doesn't mean we didn't make friendships," he said, and he took another sip of water. "Sonny was the best man at my wedding two years ago. We've worked together for years. We went to college together."

"I didn't know," I said. "I'm sorry, Adam. I saw he had an inhaler on him, but it was empty."

"I don't understand what happened," Adam said. "Sonny's asthma was never that bad. He only had the inhaler as a precaution."

"He must have overexerted himself trying to get out of that back room. He was locked in for some reason. The doorknob was on backwards or something," I explained. "I was looking… his knuckles are really beat up, like he had tried to break out."

Adam nodded. "Sonny's got bad anxiety," he said. "He might have started to hyperventilate or something. You should have heard Cher."

"You managed to get a hold of his sister?" I asked.

"Yeah. She works with us at Revival, actually. Another architect," he said. "She was the first of us to get a job at Revival out of college. She helped Sonny and I land our jobs."

Adam and I went silent. I sat next to him; I had been pacing, but I felt drained. A couple across from us were speaking loudly; the man had his arm in a sling, waiting to be seen after a bad fall.

"Didn't you hear?" the woman said. "A river of blood."

I glanced up in time to see the man roll his eyes. "Yeah, I saw it online. I think it's a hoax."

"No, I'm serious, the towns river is blood red. I saw it," she said. "There's a curse on this town. And this morning, when I was walking down Main Street, it started hailing."

"In this weather?" the man questioned. "You're out of your mind."

"Nut jobs," Adam muttered irritably. I glanced in his direction, and he sat up straight. "Sonny told me the whole town's going insane over the clocktower not working. There's a bunch of superstitious loons around here."

Before I could answer, my phone rang. I frowned when I saw it was Dustin. I really didn't have the energy for him, but I needed to let someone on the committee what had happened.

"Excuse me for a second, Adam," I said, standing up and stepping away. I made my way outside. "Dustin, you're not going to believe what kind of morning I've had…"

He didn't give me a chance to say anything more. He cut me off. "I've got bad news," he said. "About the clocktower."

"Oh, so you heard about Sonny?"

"What about him?" he questioned.

"Sonny Bono from Revival. He was found in the clocktower this morning. He had some sort of asthma attack, and he didn't make it."

"What?" Dustin exclaimed. "No, I hadn't heard. That's not what I was calling about at all... geez, Hope..."

"What's wrong with the clocktower now?" I questioned.

"The inspector just sent his report in. We're dealing with radon," he said.

"Radon!"

"Yeah," Dustin said. "We got a radon leak in the tower. The committee is having an emergency meeting tomorrow morning, and we want you there."

I groaned. "Yes, of course, I can be there. Send me the details?"

"Sure. We were going to ask Sonny to be there too, but I suppose Revival's going to need some time to figure out who they're going to send in his place," he said and then sighed. "So... what happened with Sonny exactly?"

"He somehow got himself locked into a back room. The inspector is actually the one who found him. He called 911, and the paramedics arrived. He died on the way to the hospital. I'm here now, and Adam Douglas met me over this way. He's pretty upset about the whole thing," I explained. "I think they're still trying to figure out exactly what happened. It was weird the way they found him. The backroom shouldn't have been able to lock from the outside like that, but it looked like someone had turned the doorknob around."

"That's weird," Dustin agreed. "Send Adam my condolences."

"I will," I said. "I'll see you tomorrow, Dustin."

I needed a moment to breathe before I returned to Adam. I don't know why I felt so inclined to stay, but it was probably the way Adam had looked when he arrived – so distraught. And he was by himself. Even if Adam had been unfriendly when we first met and had continued to be so, it didn't feel right leaving someone to deal with all this by themselves. But I wasn't in a rush to hurry back inside just yet either.

I took in fresh air, and then I gagged. "Ugh, what is that smell?" I groaned, covering my mouth and nose.

An ambulance had just pulled up in front of me and the medics rushed some men on gurneys into the ER. They wreaked of sulfur and looked like they had burns on their hands and faces.

"Uhg, Charlie, my eyes..." one of them cried out.

A man in a rumpled suit jumped out car nearby, but the paramedics waved him off.

"Mr. Olson, you can stay in the waiting room. We'll update you on their status," one medic said as they disappeared into the hospital entrance.

"Charlie Olson?" I asked.

The man glared at and then turned to follow the others inside. My curiosity was piqued, so I returned to the ER. Charlie yelled at the receptionist as I walked in. Adam looked up, alarmed by commotion.

The gurneys disappeared to the back, and Charlie sat down, snatching up a magazine to bury his nose in. I couldn't help myself. I walked up to Charlie Olson and stood there until he glanced up from his magazine. "Acid leak?" I asked.

He glared at me. "Back off. This is none of your concern."

"Is it the first or second one this week? Because I heard some folks whispering about the rivers turning red with blood and wanted to put that to rest," I said. "Acid colors the water red, correct?"

Charlie slapped his magazine down and stared up at me. "There was an incident yesterday as well, if you must know," he snarled. "Are you with the press or something?"

"No, I'm just a local architect," I said.

He stared at me and then a wicked looking smile crept across his face. "You're the one they're saying killed Maloney."

I nearly choked. "Excuse me?"

"Hope Wilson, right?" he asked and leaned back in his seat. "Honestly, I should shake your hand. Maloney was causing me some headaches."

Taken off guard, and I stammered. "What do you mean... I mean... who's saying that?"

"Just me," he said and then laughed at how much he had caused me to squirm. "I mean, you're the one who found the body, right? Then you're there when they find that Bono fellow."

"How could you possibly know that already?"

"Sweetheart, nothing in this town happens that I don't know about," Charlie hissed. "But it didn't take long for that story to break. It's online."

I didn't believe him, so I went back to Adam and pulled out my phone. Sure enough, a reporter had already gotten wind of what had happened at the clocktower. I was even named as being on scene. Someone had done their homework. I glanced up from my phone to see Charlie still watching me.

Adam nudged me. "Don't mess with Olson," he whispered.

I glanced at Adam. Adam wasn't even from around here, so the fact he knew Olsen's reputation was alarming. I couldn't help myself, though. If Charlie was going to stare at me like that, I was going to glare right back at him.

I felt threatened, but I refused to let him see me squirm again.

"What's the matter, sweetheart?" Charlie asked, reaching for his magazine again.

"I think we got off on the wrong foot," I said, but I'm sure my face wasn't as warm as my words. "I just met you. I apologize if I overstepped asking about the acid leak. I'm sure it's bad for your business and I know it's bad for Golden, too."

He grunted. "First impressions are everything, sweetheart."

"I'd like your permission to try again," I said, forcing my expression to relax.

This amused him, and he smirked at me from over the top of the magazine. "Very well."

"Are your employees okay?" I asked as pleasantly as I could.

"They'll be fine," he said. "There was some pressure build up thanks to a makeshift repair yesterday. We're having a hard time containing yesterday's mess, but we're doing our best."

"I'm sure," I said. "Your name has been tossed around a good bit lately. I'm curious about what you think regarding the Maloney case, since you mentioned him."

Charlie shrugged. "Sounds like he fell down the stairs. Isn't that what the police are saying?"

"It is," I said. "But I'm not sure I buy it."

"Well, your opinion isn't the one that matters, is it?" he asked.

"I suppose not," I said.

Adam's phone rang; he excused himself and stepped away as I had done before. Charlie glanced away from his reading, watching him go. "Man looks flustered," Charlie said, evidently okay with making casual conversation now.

"He and Bono went to college together, apparently," I said. "So, a little more than casual coworkers."

Charlie put on a sympathetic gaze that I suspected was a farce. "That's too bad. I made some of my closest friends in college."

"Where did you go to college, Mr. Olson?" I asked.

"UCLA. Good school."

I smiled, thinking of the class ring that was currently sitting on my nightstand. "Yes," I said. "It really is."

# Chapter Sixteen

The next morning, I was desperate to get to the police station, but I had the committee meeting. My chance run in with Charlie at the ER had proved informative. My gut told me he was behind what had happened to Maloney.

He has to be!

He admitted right there in the ER that Maloney was causing him problems. It was so arrogant of him to assume he was untouchable enough to boast about the man's demise. I was certain it was Charlie following me that night.

He had dropped his class ring!

The police couldn't overlook that.

I slipped the ring into my pocket and made my way downstairs, where Laverne was busy wrapping candies.

"That's a terrible way to go," she said after I told her about Sonny. "Poor man."

"My thoughts exactly," I said. "He was a nice guy. And I didn't like seeing his friend Adam grieving. And I certainly didn't like fibbing to the doctor either about being his fiancé. Yesterday was just an awful day in general. I heard some woman in the ER saying it hailed downtown. Did you hear about that?"

"Rivers of blood and hailstorms. The town can't stop talking about how we're cursed," Laverne snorted. "You might want to talk to your friend Tori about the hailstorms."

"Why?"

"There was some sort of accident at the tackle shop yesterday. I stopped and got me a little something to drink on my way back from my walk," Laverne explained. "Her cooling system failed, and she had to ditch the Uncle Sam sculpture. When they were moving it out, it fell and shattered in the street."

"Oh no! Tori's been working so hard on that," I said. "Well, that explains the random hailstorm. And the river of blood was probably the acid leak."

"This town and it's superstitions," Laverne said with a hand wave. "If it's not one thing, it's another. That clocktower being down has got everyone anxious. The town will only prosper so long as the clocktower is standing, as they say."

Although, I was enjoying gossiping with Aunt Laverne about the town going into mob panic, I needed to get to my meeting. I hurried out to my car. When I pulled up to city hall, there was a crowd gathered at the front steps.

"What in the world?" I muttered, stepping out and hearing the noise of panicked civilians.

"That's two deaths in one week!"

"And the cows! What about the cows?"

"My crops are going next. I just know it!"

Dustin was on the front steps alongside Tori and Bonnie, the three of them attempting to tame the crowd.

"I'm sorry, but this meeting is not open to the public," Bonnie said in a meek tone.

"We want that tower up and running now!" someone shouted.

"Please, let us have our meeting in peace," Dustin said. "This is completely out of hand."

"There is blood in the river! Tell him about the blood in the river!"

Dustin rubbed his temples. He looked desperate, and I felt inclined to act. I stepped around the mob, uttering a few forceful excuse me's to finally meet Dustin and the others at the front.

"Everyone! Please, calm down!" I shouted. "I'm the architect for the clocktower revival project. Whatever your concerns are, I'm sure—"

"Hailstorms in the middle of the day!"

"My cows!"

"What in the world?" I muttered, looking at Tori who promptly rolled her eyes and turned around on her heels to head inside.

"If you do not disperse immediately, we will call the police!" Dustin roared.

I held up a defensive hand, warning Dustin not to get the mob stirred up even further.

"We're meeting about the tower right now," I announced. "We're working on it, everyone. It's not something that can be repaired overnight. Please, go about your day, and we'll be sure to update you on the progress. Thank you."

My tone of finality helped to disperse at least some of them. As Dustin, Bonnie, and I followed Tori inside, more people departed, but we could still hear angry voices feeding off one another.

"What is going on? What are they yelling about a bunch of cows for?" I asked.

"Farmer Yuke's said half of his cows were dead in the pasture this morning," Tori said.

"What!" I yelped. "Are you serious? Don't they have one of the biggest cow farms in the county?"

"Fifty-two dead cows," Bonnie said.

"Fifty-two!" I exclaimed. "That's nothing to scoff about."

"No, it's not," Tori said. "But everyone is losing their minds like they think the end times are upon us."

"I heard about the ice sculpture," Bonnie said.

"Yeah, there are rumors going around it was a hailstorm in the middle of a sunny day. And Charlie Olson is happily letting people spin the whole river of blood nonsense because it takes attention off the fact that there were two acid leaks in the past two days," Dustin said, looking just as irritated as Tori.

"The acid leaks are probably what killed the cattle," I said. "Doesn't the river run through Yuke's property? His cows have probably been drinking from the river for days."

"I'm sure," Tori said. "Yuke should have gotten his cattle away from the river when word about the acid leak got out, but he didn't. That's his own fault. He's lucky the entire herd isn't dead."

"Let's just get to the meeting, the others are waiting," Bonnie said, marching ahead of us.

Sharron and Ted were already waiting in the meeting room. Ted glanced up as we entered, and he grinned. "Did you manage to scare the town nuts away, Dustin?" he asked.

Dustin rolled his eyes. "Some are leaving, but there's still a good group of them out there. They're not going to be happy with what we've decided."

I glanced in Tori's direction; she avoided eye contact with me. "What you've decided?" I asked. "What do you mean? I thought we were here to discuss the radon leak in the clocktower."

"The radon leak is only one obstacle," Dustin said, sitting down at the table. The others joined him, and he motioned me to do the same. "Two people have died in that tower in the past week and a half. The townsfolk are completely losing their minds. I spoke with Sherriff James this morning, and Sonny Bono's death was more than just an asthma attack."

"What? What was it?" I questioned.

"According to the autopsy report, the level of radon in his lungs was astronomical."

"You're joking!" I said. "Radon is dangerous, sure, but it's cancerous. It's not going to choke a person out."

"Tell that to Sonny Bono," Dustin said. "There was a secondary chemical in his system. Carbon monoxide."

"Great," I said. "So now we're dealing with radon and carbon monoxide gas. Well, that's nothing we can't fix. How severe a leak are we dealing with?"

"Severe enough that we've decided to have the whole place condemned," he said.

My jaw dropped and the world seemed to tilt.

"I'm sorry, what? You're going to tear down the clocktower? Dustin, what happened to renovation!"

"Come on, Hope," Ted muttered. "You know as well as we do that those are some pretty serious problems. We don't even know where to find the carbon monoxide leak. The inspector didn't include it in his report. Who knows what other monstrosities are hidden in that thing?"

"So what am I doing here?" I snapped. "If you all decided to condemn the place then why have me come to this meeting?"

"The clocktower housed one of Golden's satellite receivers," Tori said, still avoiding my eyes.

I glanced in her direction, and I seethed when she averted her eyes.

Thanks for the heads up, buddy.

"We need an architect to supervise its removal and relocation. We'd like for you to oversee it. We know you've spent a lot of time and energy preparing for this project, so we felt it only fair to offer you the job first," Tori said.

I stared at them in disbelief as the voices outside started to rise. "You all hear that too, don't you? When word gets out that you're condemning that building—"

"There's nothing we can do, Hope," Dustin insisted.

I stood. "I'll do whatever you guys need me to do," I said. "But I think you're making a terrible mistake."

I stormed out of the building, my heart shattered into a million pieces.

It was not about losing the job; it had never really been about the job. It was about saving something that meant the world to me and to Steven and heck, the entire town of Golden.

Now, the clocktower was going to be torn down and there was nothing I could do about.

I sped back to Aunt Laverne's, completely forgetting to speak with the police about Olson.

# Chapter Seventeen

The following day, I started making the calls about the satellite receiver relocation. We set a date for just after the Butter and Egg parade, and then I was going to get one final hoorah in Golden before I flew the coop. I planned to leave town once the job was done. There was no way I could justify staying in town waiting for the committee to get funding for the museum renovation or the miner statue. Those projects were yet to be funding and if their future was in doubt, I needed a plan to feed myself.

I packed between phone calls.

I sighed as I closed my suitcase. The zipper sounded like nails on a chalkboard. It was like a carrot had been dangled in front of me. I had finally decided to come back to Golden, but now there wasn't any reason for me to stay. My phone buzzed, and I sighed, expecting it to be a follow up call about the satellite.

"Hope, hon!" The strong LA-valley voice surprised me.

"Cort?" Cortney and I were acquaintances from back in LA. She was a fellow architect, further along in her career than me. We'd always had friendly competition, snatching clients up that the other wanted.

"Hey, Golden Girl," she sang. "Whatcha up to?"

"Not a whole lot," I said. "I'm in Golden at the moment."

"Really? Golden Girl went back home? Don't tell me you've gone back to small town life.," she teased.

I rolled my eyes. "What do you want, Cort?"

"I got a little surprise for you. I'm guessing if you're in Golden, I'm not going to be able to give you the news in person, so..."

"So you don't get to spend twenty minutes playing around with me. What's up?" I asked.

"You sound like you're in a foul mood."

"Cort!" I groaned.

"All right, fine. I overbooked this spring, and as much as I would like to juggle a million projects, I'm not superwoman. An architectural firm out in Chicago, a personal favorite of yours, is looking for a modern sky-rise building. Your style, hon. I showed them your portfolio because, as painful as it is for me to admit it, this one suits you a lot more than it does me."

I was on the floor dragging out shoes that had been kicked underneath the bed when Cortney broke the news to me. I bolted upright. "I'm sorry, you did what?"

"You heard me. Chicago Cornerstone Architectural Associates wants you, doll face," Cortney said. "All you got to do is sign. My assistant will email you the contract today."

"You... you got me a design job in Chicago with Cornerstone?" I barely choked out my surprise.

"I did, lovely," Cortney said. "And I'd say that one earned me a night out with you when you get back to LA."

"Cort, I swear, if you're pulling my leg right now, the first thing I do when I get back is knock you out and bury your body in the dessert."

"I'm not joking, you loser," Cortney said. "Check your email. It's legit, and when you're done being sassy, you can tell me how much you love me and can't wait to see me in LA next week, because we're going clubbing. I have to go. I have other clients to attend, and I can't spend all day on the phone with some small-town hick."

"Cute," I muttered, but I smiled. "Cortney, thank you."

"Anytime, Golden Girl."

Cortney hung up the phone, and I sat—or rather threw myself—onto the bed. I pulled up my email. It was exactly as Cortney had said: a job offer with the Chicago Cornerstone Architectural Associates. I'd wanted to work with them for years. If I could impress them with a sky-rise design, I might would be looking at a permanent position. They were known for finding freelance architects like myself and bringing them onto the team permanently if they impressed. They never took resumes or applications; they found you, and if they liked what you're designs you were set for life. This could be the career-changing project that catapulted me beyond my wildest dreams.

"Yes! Yes!" I wailed, just as a text message came through from Tori.

I'm sorry I didn't get a chance to talk to you before the meeting yesterday.

I took a deep breath, then I called her. She sounded so upset when she answered the phone. "I'm so glad you called!" she exclaimed. "I owe you a huge apology."

"It's fine, Tori," I said.

"No!" she said. "I should have told you what the committee was planning on doing yesterday, but things have been crazy at the tackle shop after the ice sculpture started melting, and when we tried to move it —"

"I heard you caused a hailstorm," I teased, and Tori exhaled with relief. She knew I wasn't angry.

"No, I did not cause a hailstorm," she said. "I really am sorry. I should have called you and told you the second they started talking like they weren't going to go through with the renovation, but I was so wrapped up in my own stuff. I'm sorry, Hope."

"It's okay, Tori, really," I said. "Besides, I'm starting to think it was for the best. I just got a call from a connection in LA, and she got me a job offer with this firm out in Chicago. I'm looking over the contract now and…" I paused, realizing the line had gotten painfully quiet. "Tori?"

"You got a job offer in Chicago," she said flatly.

"Yes, with Chicago Cornerstone Architectural Associates. They're one of the most prestigious architectural firms around, and they want me. Can you believe it?" My excitement faded; she was too quiet. "Tori?" I beckoned.

"It's exciting," she said, sounding anything but excited. "Hope… are you leaving?"

I instinctually glanced around the room. "Well… I mean…"

"You're running away again."

That triggered me. A fury rose up inside me so quickly I could hardly contain it. "Is that what you think?" I snapped. "No, I'm just not happy here, Tori, I never have been. Not since Steven died, at least. This place smothers me."

"No, it doesn't," Tori said matter-of-factly. "You were so happy. I could see it in your eyes, and you put so much work into that proposal. I mean, seriously? You wanted this job bad because you love this town, and you were glad to be back. But now it just got a little hard, and you're ready to run away again."

"No, that's not it!" I shouted. "I'm not like you, Tori. I'm not happy being some small-town mommy. That's not me. I've got bigger plans for myself than running my parent's old beer and bait shop." I crossed a line. I bit my bottom lip and tried to step back. "I didn't mean it like that."

"No, I know you didn't," she said, but she sounded furious. "And that's the problem. I saw Laverne yesterday. She told me you still haven't gone to see Steven's parents. You planning on leaving without seeing them, Hope?"

"I've been busy. Of course I'll go see them before I—"

"Yeah, right," Tori said. "You're just running away again. You know what? You weren't the only person hurting, Hope. Steven was my friend too! And screw you for leaving us to deal with that on our own without you." She hung up on me.

I tried to call her back, but the phone didn't even ring. She'd shut her phone off, and I couldn't blame her. I had overstepped. And while she had been harsh, I knew it was something I had needed to hear. Tears escaped me, but I wiped them away. I wasn't going to sulk. It was time I sucked it up.

The class ring I found the night I ran into Peter was sitting on my nightstand. There were a few things I needed to do if I was going to leave

Golden for Chicago. Reporting Charlie Olson to the police was one thing. Going to see Steven's parents was another.

I grabbed the ring from the nightstand and tucked it into my pocket, then made my way downstairs. Laverne was nowhere to be seen, so I figured she was out for her afternoon walk. There were a few candies unwrapped, and I spent a little bit of time wrapping them before leaving the house.

I drove through town, my heart beating a million miles an hour, deciding to hit up the police station on my way back. There was one thing I needed to do first before anything else.

I needed to see Steven's parents.

# Chapter Eighteen

The house was exactly as I remembered it: a modest place on a large corner lot. They bought it shortly after Steven and I started dating, and we helped them move in. We bought pizza, and me and Mr. Wilson sat on the front porch drinking lemonade.

"So, young lady, what are your intentions with my son?" he asked, and I laughed at Steven's embarrassment.

Now, I could almost see Steven in that front lawn, tossing a football back and forth with his father. They'd always been close, and that had left room for me to get close to Mrs. Wilson. She adored me, and I'd betrayed them by not visiting sooner.

With a deep breath, I made my way to the house. Sure, I'd spoken to them on the phone a handful of times, but that wasn't what they needed. I had to make amends; Tori had been right to scold me.

I was about to knock when I heard the lawn mower making its way around to the front of the house. I smiled, remembering when Mr. Wilson bought the ride-on mower. He was exceptionally proud of his yards. He had insisted on getting an enormous zero turn mower. It was way too much for the yard, of course, but it made him feel like he really accomplished something.

I made my way to the side of the porch, ready to greet the man as he came around. I stopped dead in my tracks when I saw it was not Mr. Wilson.

It was Dustin.

"The hell..." I muttered as the mower came to a slow and winding stop.

Dustin muttered under his breath about gas. He hadn't seen me yet, so I slowly backed up.

Why is he here?

"Hope!" I was startled by a woman's voice, and I turned to see Mrs. Wilson at the front door. Her face had positively lit up, and her eyes filled with tears as she darted in my direction.

She nearly knocked me over, and she pulled me into her arms. Dustin climbed off the mower, and looked in our direction with a scowl.

"Out of gas," he muttered. "I'm going to see if there's any more in the barn."

Mrs. Wilson held me so tightly it was almost a chokehold. "It's good to see you too," I said, and I wiped away a tear. "I'm so sorry."

"Sorry?" she questioned, releasing me at last. "For what?"

"I've been so distant," I said. "I mean, I've been in town for a bit now, and I haven't even called. I was afraid to come see you because we haven't spoken much, and I feel so guilty."

"Come inside," she said, not allowing me to say another word.

I followed her, glancing back toward the abandoned lawn mower before entering the house. She ushered me into the kitchen and poured me a glass of lemonade. I smiled; I'd missed her lemonade. Her husband always joked about it being a southern woman's lemonade because of the amount of sugar she put into it, but we all knew he secretly loved it as much as anyone else.

"Thank you," I said, and I sat down at the kitchen island. Even the kitchen reminded me of Steven. How many times had we come over for breakfast with his folks?

"Let me go get Jerald," she said. "He's going to be so happy to see you, Hope." And with that, she left me alone.

I took a few deep breaths, realizing I was okay. Yes, this place brought back a lot of memories, but they were happy ones. Mrs. Wilson took her time getting back with her husband, so I wandered into the living room. Across the mantlepiece were framed pictures, the largest being mine and Steven's wedding photo. It didn't hurt quite as much as I thought it would.

Actually, I smiled at first. I placed my lemonade on the mantle, picking up the photo and staring at it. He looked so handsome in his suit, and the way he was looking at me brought a lump to my throat.

"Jerald, I'm going to have to run down and get gas, I'll be...." Dustin's voice cut off. Of course, he had caught me just as I was getting worked up.

I panicked, desperate to wipe my face, and I put the photo back too quickly, completely forgetting about the lemonade. I knocked it clear off the mantle, and it shattered everywhere. "Ack!"

"Hold on, I got you." Dustin hurried to the kitchen, returning with a dish towel. We both went to the ground, hurriedly picking up glass. "Careful," he warned me, cleaning up the lemonade before it dripped from the fireplace to the carpet.

I wiped my eyes on the back of my sleeve, and the next thing I knew he had his arm around me, pulling me into an embrace. I hadn't expected sympathy from Dustin, and it took everything I had not to get myself worked up again. I exhaled deeply twice before letting go, feeling like I had my bearings again.

We picked up the rest of the glass and threw it into the kitchen trash. Dustin rinsed out the dish towel.

"What are you doing here, Dustin?"

"Cutting the grass."

"You don't say." I crossed my arms.

"Would you stop pouting every time we run into each other?" he demanded, wringing out the rag. He turned around to face me. "Sandra's got arthritis in her wrists, says it's been hurting pretty bad for a couple of years now. Then last year, Jerald pulled his back out. They're stubborn about letting me help around here, but they need it. Now, if you will excuse me, I need to go get gas for the mower." He started to turn away from me, but I reached out and grabbed his arm. "What?" he snapped.

"Thank you."

He jerked his arm away from me. "Yeah, well, someone had to help them out." He stormed out of the house, slamming the front door.

"I heard something break!" Mr. Wilson called, and I darted into the living room. He grinned at me from the hallway, shoveling along with a walker. "Say one word, darling, and I'll knock you over with it," he warned me.

I grinned at him. "That thing makes you look ten years older than you are, you old fart."

He laughed, shuffling into the living room and holding out an arm toward me. I hurried to hug him tight. "I'm so sorry," I told him.

"Oh, you shut up," the old man warned me. "Help me over to my chair, would you?"

Mrs. Wilson wasn't far behind. She moved the walker out of the way, and I helped her husband into a large chair in the corner. "I'm so sorry about the glass, Sandra," I said. "Dustin came in and surprised me, and I dropped it on the fireplace."

"Looks like you managed to miss the carpet," she said with a grin. "It's fine, Hope. I'll get you another. I know you like my lemonade."

"Rots your teeth," Mr. Wilson said. His wife popped him in the back of the head as she walked by, but the playfulness made him grin even wider.

"I see you're not letting a bad back slow you down," I said, sitting on the corner of the nearby couch so that I could be close to him. "I've really missed you guys. I'm sorry that I—"

"Stop saying you're sorry," he said. "Hope, I understand, sweetheart. You have your life to live. I'm just really glad to see you."

Mrs. Wilson reappeared with a glass of lemonade, which she handed to me, and her husband looked at her expectantly. "Oh, so you do want some of my sugar water, then?" she questioned and shook her head, returning to the kitchen to get her husband a glass.

Their friendly banter was certainly something I had missed. Steven and I were like that too. He grew up in a home with parents who had never stopped finding one another attractive, which resulted in some humiliating stories from him, but it had turned him into a truly loving husband himself.

I sat with them talking and catching up long enough for Dustin to return and finish cutting grass outside. It must have given him the space he needed to cool off because he was all smiles now, listening to me talk about my upcoming project in Chicago and a million other things.

"Miss Hollywood over here," he teased after joining us in the living room. "You should have seen her in the committee meeting. She was a show off."

"Oh, I bet," Mr. Wilson said. "I've seen some of those buildings you designed in LA. Not in person, but I keep up with you online."

"You? Online?" I questioned.

"I'm not that old," he retorted. "Oh, show Hope the scrapbook you've made, Sandra."

Sandra beamed proudly at her husband's recognition, and she scurried over to the bookshelf in the corner, opening the bottom cabinet. She sat between Dustin and I, and she opened a scrapbook that positively melted my heart. There were newspaper articles and printouts of the buildings I had been on design committees for.

"You made this?" I asked, taking the scrapbook from her. "Oh... Mrs. Wilson..." I felt so touched.

"We like to keep up with what our Hope is doing," she said. "Even if she doesn't call to update us herself."

"Sandra!" Mr. Wilson snapped. "Don't go giving her a hard time."

"Somebody should," Dustin said. He jerked as a tennis ball hit him in the head.

I glanced in Mr. Wilson's direction. He had yanked one of the tennis balls from the bottom of his walker and tossed it at Dustin. I bit my bottom lip, and Mrs. Wilson burst into a fit of laughter at Dustin's surprised expression. He quickly relented.

"Sorry," he muttered, a smile escaping him. "Well, I should probably go put the mower in the barn. I'll be back in a sec." He jumped up and headed out.

I looked at the time. I really needed to go talk to Sheriff James. "I'll be sure to come by again before I leave Golden," I promised them, and they looked sad when I said this. "And," I added, "I promise not to go so long without seeing you guys again. Or talking."

They smiled at me, and Mrs. Wilson saw me to the door. I sighed heavily as I made my way down the porch steps. "Leaving?" Dustin appeared from the side of the house.

"Yeah," I said. "I need to go by the sheriff's station before I go back to your aunt's to finish packing."

Dustin looked at me quizzically. "Sheriff's station?"

"I found some evidence they'll be interested in," I said and pulled out the class ring. "I found this the night I was confronted on my way back to Laverne's. Turns out, Charlie Olson studied at the UCLA. I think he was the one threatening me, and he has a motive too. Maloney was suing him over working conditions in your dad's mine."

Dustin raised a brow, and I handed him the ring to look at. "I never heard of any lawsuit."

"It didn't go through," I said. "Maloney was the one pushing it, and after he was killed, it looks like it got dropped."

"Charlie Olson isn't someone you want to be messing with, Hope," he said. "Look, he's just some uppity goldmine manager. And this isn't his ring."

"How would you know that?" I asked.

"I know Olson pretty well," Dustin said. "Saw him just yesterday, and he was wearing his stupid class ring."

"What?" Dustin handed the ring back to me.

"Yeah, he was wearing it. We got to talking about college football, and he showed it to me," Dustin said. "So, that's not his ring. You want to know what I think? I think you're just trying to stir up trouble because you're disappointed about the clocktower."

"Are you serious?" I stuffed the ring back into my pocket. "Dustin, you can't possibly believe I'm that childish. Someone threatened me! And t wo people are dead!"

"I don't know what happened to Wayne Maloney or what he was doing in the clocktower in the first place, but Sonny Bono breathed in some dangerous gasses and had an asthma attack. That has nothing to do with what happened to Maloney."

"Sonny Bono was locked in a room he couldn't escape from," I said. "And the inspector couldn't find any evidence of carbon monoxide, yet it was found in Sonny's system. I think someone killed Sonny."

"You're delirious," Dustin said, waving a hand in my direction.

My shoulders tensed and I opened my mouth to spout Lord knows what in his direction, but Mrs. Wilson appeared on the front porch. "Hope!" she beckoned.

Dustin and I glared at one another for a moment more before I broke away and went to see what Mrs. Wilson needed. She had the scrapbook in her arms, grinning at me as I approached. "I just wanted to loan you this, in case you wanted to finish looking through it? You can return it before you have to leave for Chicago."

"Thank you so much," I said, and I gave her one last hug. I tucked the scrapbook under my arm. She returned to the house, and when I turned back to my car, Dustin had stormed off again.

I sighed as I got into my car. I placed the scrapbook on the passenger's seat and pulled out. Part of me still wanted to go by the sheriff's station to talk to them about the class ring, but what was the point? I doubted Dustin lied about seeing Charlie Olson's own ring, and as far as I knew, the ring I had wasn't going to connect me to anyone else.

There were other things I needed to take care of before leaving town though, and the Butter and Egg parade was approaching fast. Instead of going to the station, I headed to the beer and tackle shop to visit Tori. I needed to make things right with her sooner rather than later.

# Chapter Nineteen

The Butter and Egg parade was upon us, and my days in Golden were numbered. I hadn't been to one of these things in five years, and I was actually looking forward to it.

I met Tori at the bait and tackle shop. After the disaster that had ended her Uncle Sam sculpture, she had gone into overtime creating a new one for the parade. A life-size Uncle Sam was too much to recreate with the time limitations. Instead, she did a chicken and nest. It didn't require as many details as Uncle Sam would have.

"Whoa," I said when I entered the tackle shop's freezer behind her. "You actually managed to pull it off. I'm impressed."

Tori grinned. "What can I say? I'm a pro. And, thank you so much for offering to help me get it into the truck."

"Anytime," I said. We grabbed hold of the slings she had wrapped around the thing. There was a large wooden plank in the center of the room with rollers on the bottom. This was how we intended to move the sculpture outside. It was the same way she had been moving Uncle Sam when it had fallen and shattered, so I was nervous.

We managed to get it onto the plank, and from that point it was simple.

"Easy," Tori said about every three seconds as we rolled it through the shop and out the front door.

"I'm being as easy as I can be, Tori," I said.

It was cold just being near the thing. We wore gloves, but my fingers were still freezing by the time we made it to her van.

It was a small white van stationed out front that Tori used for moving her sculptures. She had hired a graffiti artist to put the company logo on the side instead of having the thing professionally wrapped. She opened the double doors, and we rolled the sculpture right up to the back, each gripping tight onto the slings.

"One... two... three!" Tori shrieked louder than necessary, but I suppose the extra volume provided the motivational umph we needed. We barely managed to get it up onto the back of the truck, but once we did it slid in very easily.

"You're the best!" Tori said.

My back cracked when I stood upright again, and Tori cringed in my direction. I laughed it off. "I'll send you my doctor bill," I said.

"Heck no," Tori said. "I know you. You'll go to some fancy LA doc when you get back home. You pay for that yourself."

I smiled, shaking my head as we made our way around the van and climbed inside

"Oy!" Tori said as she started up the van. She punched the small generator between us to get the freezer system going.

"Nicely done," I said, and we pulled off.

There was an excessive amount of traffic in Golden that day. The Butter and Egg parade always brought in tourists, and the streets were packed with vendors galore, all hoping to promote their local shops and businesses. We drove to city hall where Tori checked her ice sculpture into the parade and handed it off.

"I'm just glad they were okay with going from a giant Uncle Sam to the chicken and nest," Tori said after we parked and made our way to the street.

"I'm impressed you were able to pull that off so quickly," I said.

Tori yawned. "It wasn't easy. But now I can relax and take in the event. Hubby will be by later with the kiddo once he's up from his nap and… and there it goes…" Her phone had started ringing.

"Husband calling with a Nolan emergency?" I asked.

"I'm sure," she said. "You go ahead; I'll catch up with you." She walked back to the car, muttering something about keeping crayons out of their son's reach.

I checked out the vendor booths. I didn't make it far before I spotted Charlie Olson in the crowd. He had a table set up promoting the mining company, clearly hoping to get the attention of potential investors and clients.

"I'm telling you, folks, I'll will hook you up with a deal like nobody else," he said to a handful of interested and important-looking gentleman.

He looked so smug, and I wanted to get a closer look at his hand to confirm what Dustin had said about his class ring.

"That's awfully fine of you to be offering a good deal to new clients," I said as I approached the table. "But what would it look like for your investors if another lawsuit comes up surrounding your miner working conditions?"

He shot daggers at me with his eyes.

"You're talking like we've been sued before, Miss," he said. "Which has never happened. This is a local here just trying to make trouble, I assure you all." He passed out some pamphlets and then excused himself, walking around the table toward me.

I thought he was just going to say something snarky under his breath, but he actually snatched me by the arm.

"Hey!" I said as he jerked me toward the parking lot.

He shoved me back and jabbed a finger in my face. "You pull a stunt like that again, woman, and I swear you will never forget my face."

"Too late, it's already ingrained in my brain—scarred," I snapped. He came toward me, a crazed look in his eye that, for a split second, made me afraid, like he was going to hit me.

"Back up," Dustin snarled, appearing from behind Charlie and grabbing the man at the shoulder. He spun Charlie around, and Dustin looked twice as crazed as Charlie.

"Mr. Peterson," Charlie said casually, as though he hadn't just accosted me. "You'd better let me handle this. This has nothing to do with you."

"I'm not going anywhere," Dustin snarled. "If I ever see you treat another human being like that again, you can rest assured your job at my father's mine will be in jeopardy. Go back to the table. You're supposed to be working."

Charlie gritted his teeth, but he stalked away. As he went, I got a glimpse of his hand. He had a ring. Dang it!

"Are you all right?" Dustin asked.

"I'm fine," I said and smiled at him. "Thank you."

Dustin's face relax, his jaw unclenching after the interaction with Olson.

"What are you doing, Hope?" he asked. There was a calmness to his voice that I hadn't heard since I had arrived back in Golden.

"What do you mean?"

"What did you say to Charlie," he said. "Are you still looking into what happened to Maloney? Even though you're leaving Golden?"

I fidgeted. "Somebody should be looking into it, right?"

"Would you stay in Golden?" he asked.

I stared back at him. "I'm sorry?"

"Would you stay if you could? I mean, are you disappointed about the clocktower just because it was something important to you and Steven, or are you disappointed because you have to leave?" he asked.

"What are you asking me, Dustin?"

He looked sad. "I just want to know if you would stay. If you want to stay or if you really were just here for a job. Did you want to stay, Hope?"

I wasn't sure what to say, but I was saved by his phone ringing. He glanced down and sighed. "Aunt Laverne. She needs me to come help transport the candy here."

"Go ahead and answer it."

"You're leaving tomorrow, aren't you?" he asked.

"That's the plan."

"Promise me you'll meet up with me later to talk? Please?"

I nodded. "Okay. I promise."

He put the phone to his ear, hurrying off. "Yes, I'm on my way…"

I watched him go. He had wanted to tell me something, but I couldn't piece together what he had been getting at.

*Does he want me to stay in Golden?*

After all the tension between us in the past weeks, what had changed?

It was then I realized I had left my wallet back at Laverne's. The Butter and Egg festival was a great time to get a good deal on just about anything that was sold locally, so I shot Tori a quick text letting her know I was going to walk back to the house and that I would meet up with her later. I could have asked Dustin to pick it up for me while he was there, but something was holding me back.

He'd been implying something I still hadn't fully grasped, so I made the short walk to Laverne's from downtown, completely oblivious to the person following me.

# Chapter Twenty

When I arrived at the house, Dustin's truck was in the driveway. I was hoping I'd pass him on the way so I didn't bump into him here. I entered the house, and sure enough Dustin was in the kitchen with Aunt Laverne, putting boxes of treats into wooden crates.

"What are you doing here?" he asked, but his tone lacked the hostility I'd grown used to from him. If anything, it sounded friendly.

"I left my wallet," I explained.

"Well, that's no good!" Aunt Laverne said. "With all the booths at the festival, you're bound to find at least one thing you want to throw your money at."

"Ain't that the truth," I said, excusing myself and hurrying up the stairs. I looked around for my wallet for what felt like an eternity, but it was nowhere to be seen. "Weird," I said with a groan.

It occurred to me that I could have left it in my car, so I headed back downstairs. Laverne and Dustin had made their way outside as well. Laverne was in the passenger's seat of the truck, and Dustin was loading the last of the crates of candy.

"Find your wallet?" he asked.

"No, not yet. I'm thinking I left it in my car," I explained. He looked like he had something he wanted to say, but he kept quiet. "So, I'll see you at the parade?" I said, and he nodded, jumping in the truck and driving off with his aunt.

Something weird is going on with him.

I opened my car door and spied the scrapbook Mrs. Wilson had lent me. The wallet was underneath it. I picked it up, but I paused at the sight of the scrapbook.

I slipped into my passengers' seat and opened the scrapbook in my lap, smiling. It had been such a sweet gesture. I flipped through the pages, pausing to look at some of the articles Mrs. Wilson had cut out of various LA papers. One of the articles slid off the page, the glue coming loose.

"Oh, shoot!" I snagged the loose newspaper clipping before it could fall out of my open car door.

It was a picture of the office complex I worked on when I first arrived in Los Angeles, and my heart warmed. It was one of my earliest projects. The article covered the building's grand opening; it had been a proud moment.

I turned the clipping over to examine where the glue had come loose when an article heading on the back caught my eye: University of California, Los Angeles Alumni Celebrates 30 Years at JW Marriott.

The article listed the alumni members who had orchestrated the event about two years ago, and the name Sanders popped up. It wasn't Mark Sanders, of course, but the name Gregory Sanders sounded painfully familiar.

"Mark's dad graduated from the UCLA?" I questioned.

From what I could remember, old Gregory Sanders passed away last year. I didn't attend the funeral because I hadn't known the guy, but I'd seen a few Golden friends posting about it. Gregory had been a big guy compared to his son, Mark, but the two had been close.

The last I saw the class ring, I was in the car, and I slipped it into the cup holder. I reached out to grab it, wondering what class year had been engraved on the ring. My hand fiddled around in the cup holder, but it wasn't there.

"Weird," I muttered leaning over the drivers' seat to see if it had fallen, but as I did, a strong hand reached into the car and grabbed me by my hair.

He yanked me from the car, and I screamed. He released my hair once I was outside, but was still squaring up at me.

"Mark!" I exclaimed in surprise, seeing Mark Sanders in front of me. I reached and touched my head.

"You should have kept your mouth shut and minded your own business like I said," he scowled. The ring was back on his finger. My mistake had been assuming the ring's owner had actually gone to the UCLA and not been an heirloom.

"Back off," I warned, but he looked crazed.

Fear shot up my spine. I knew this wasn't going to end well.

He came at me. I jumped back and gave my car's door a solid kick. It swung on him, and a ting sounded loudly as the door collided with the ring.

"Ya!" he hollered, but the impacted only slowed him down momentarily.

I ran toward the street, and he was right on my heels.

"I'm going to kill you," he growled. "You were the one who was supposed to die, not that other architect. It should have been you!"

Mark grabbed my arm as we reached the middle of the street, and he pulled me back, his arms going around my waist and jerking me up off the ground.

I flung an elbow back, hitting him in the nose, and he let go. The roar of engine filled my ears and I looked up just in time to see a truck barreling down the street at us.

I leaped out of the way, nearly colliding headfirst with the pavement, I ducked my head into my arms and skinned my elbows on the asphalt.

"Watch out!" a man shouted.

Rolling over onto my back, I looked up in time to see the truck strike Mark. He flew through the air, thumping his head hard on the street.

The driver jumped out. It was Laverne, behind the wheel of Dustin's truck.

"You little creep!" Laverne shouted as Dustin jumped from the passenger's side.

Dustin ran around to me, helping me up. I was confused. Dustin was driving away not ten minutes before. But it didn't matter. Laverne was over by Mark, and I swear I saw her give him a kick with her shoe; he groaned in response.

"He's fine," she said, "I only bumped him."

"Are you all right?" Dustin asked, wide-eyed. "We saw him grab you, and... well... Aunt Laverne rammed the gas..."

Laverne had her cellphone out and was on the phone with the police, making the situation sound twice as dramatic as it actually was, although truth be told I was a bit shaken up.

"I'm fine," I told Dustin. "But I'm pretty sure he's the one who chased me down the other night."

"But why?" Dustin asked.

I shook my head. I could hardly believe Peter figured it out before I did. "Peter was right. This wasn't about the lawsuit. It was about Belinda Johnson. Mark got into a fight with Wayne at the tavern the night Wayne was killed. And Mark just said something about Sonny too. He was going after me, but Sonny wound up at the clocktower that day instead of me. He must have heard I was the one working the clocktower remodel and didn't expect someone else to be there. He was trying to get me to stop looking into things."

"That's why the door handle had been turned around, and he somehow filled the room with carbon monoxide fumes," Dustin said. "He had planned to kill you, Hope." Dustin's voice was raspy.

Mark let out another groan as we the sirens approached. Within minutes, Mark was on a stretcher while Sheriff James stood with Dustin, Laverne, and me on the sidewalk, scratching his head and trying to figure out what had taken place.

"So that I'm clear," he began. "You're telling me Mark followed Wayne after he left the tavern and killed him at the clocktower. And then he overheard you chatting with Peter Lentz and got nervous when his name was dropped as a suspect and decided to try to kill you, but instead he got Sonny Bono?"

"That's what I'm thinking," I said. "I'm just glad he didn't go after Peter first." The thought of Steven's young companion being hurt by that creep made me sick. "Only thing I haven't pieced together yet is the bank statements I found of Wayne's. I can't imagine who was sending him such large sums of cash."

"I might be able to answer that one," Dustin said reluctantly. "Charlie Olson's poor management at the mines has gotten him into a boat of trouble. There have been too many accidents lately. The back-to-back acid leaks earlier this week are just the latest in his screw ups. My dad started encouraging people to buy Olson's shares in the gold mines, and I happen to know Belinda was doing investments for some of her clients. Wayne was one of them. I saw her the other day at my dad's office talking about cashing out some of the shares for his family."

James nodded; the look on his face telling me there was some serious epiphany taking place. "So Belinda, Mark, and Wayne were working together to sue and slander Olson in an attempt to take his stake in E-Goldrush.com. Apparently encouraged by your father, Dustin. But Wayne and Belinda got a little too close for Mark's comfort."

"Exactly," I said. "And I'll bet you anything Mark wanted to keep the entire share and was trying to push out Wayne. Maybe he would have even gone after Belinda too if things escalated. The money in Wayne's account was probably thanks to some of the company shares he invested in."

"Well, we'll let the police piece together the details," James said. "But I'm glad you're okay, Hope. This could have gotten nasty quickly."

"No thanks to you," Laverne said, and James glared in her direction.

"I'm going to let that comment slide," James said. "And not arrest you for trying to run a man over with a truck."

Laverne smirked. "I was only going five miles an hour, and it was self defense."

"Self defense?" James asked.

"Yeah!" Laverne helped. "I was acting in self-defense for Hope."

James nodded. "Right. The law of defense of others," he mumbled as he made a note in his notebook. He put the notebook away, then waved at us as he left with the other officers, following the ambulance to the hospital.

"Well," Laverne said, brushing herself off. "I'm going to take the truck back to the festival before the parade starts. I'll get the last of those candies unloaded. Meet me there, Dustin."

When he started to protest, she wagged her finger at him and left him there without a ride.

I laughed at finding myself alone with Dustin on the sidewalk where Laverne had nearly plowed me not half an hour before.

"I'm lucky you two showed up when you did," I said. "But, if you weren't finished with unloading the candies, why were you guys headed back here anyways?"

Dustin's face went red. "You know Aunt Laverne, always got to have things her way."

"I'm sorry?"

He rolled his eyes at me, looking flustered. After a deep exhale, he gave me the real answer. "I was talking to her about... what I wanted to talk to you about earlier... and she practically shoved me into the truck and decided it couldn't wait and dragged me back here."

That sounded like Laverne. "And what is it you wanted to talk to me about earlier, Dustin?"

He rubbed the back of his head, interlocking his fingers and huffing, trying and failing to hide his nerves. "Why can't you stay?" he asked.

"Why can't I stay? Meaning here in Golden? I don't know, maybe because you're having the clocktower condemned?"

Dustin rolled his eyes and lowered his arms. "Is the clocktower the only reason you came back to Golden, Hope? For a job? Or did you miss being here?"

I started to tell him no, but he looked at me with those sad eyes, and I knew I needed to start being honest with him as well as myself.

"I missed home," I admitted.

He smiled and released a long exhale. "Okay," he said. "So, I was speaking with Bonnie and Ted this morning, and they weren't really sold on the idea of condemning the clocktower, and I know Tori wasn't either. I decided to schedule a follow-up meeting tomorrow to discuss saving it, and I really hope you would reconsider being our architect."

I think an explosion went off in my head. "I'm sorry?" I asked, my tone harsh, and that was clearly not the reaction he had been expecting.

"You're... you're mad?" he gawked.

"Yeah, I'm mad!" I shouted. "Because where has this attitude been the whole time? Dustin, I just got a job offer from Chicago, and it's a good one—career changing! And now you're wanting to save the clocktower? Now? Dustin Graham Peterson, I could strangle you!"

My tone must have softened toward the end of my rant because the smile on that man's face was almost too much for me.

"Are you going to stay?" he asked, even though I had said no such thing.

"Why do you want me to stay? You've been trying to get me out of town since the day I got back."

Dustin smiled in response to my anger. "That day we were with the Wilsons... listening to you talk about Steven with them again... I know I popped off at you and I shouldn't have, but I went home thinking about it. About how much I've missed that. Missed your stupid humor and hanging out with you and with Steven even though I couldn't stand you."

"Gee, thanks."

"I've missed you, Hope," he said. "I really, really missed you. And I'm not the only one. Did you know the clocktower stopped working the day you left Golden?"

I stared at him. "It did? That can't be right. I thought it only stopped working a few weeks ago."

"The first time around I was able to fix it," he said. "But, I swear, it's like this whole town has been on some dramatic pause since you left. Like we've all just been living the same day over and over. I'm still mad at you for leaving, but I don't want you to do it again. Please, consider staying. I'm going to talk to the committee, and I think they'll all be on board once we get a follow-up inspection, especially if we learn that the carbon monoxide thing was all Mark and not some problem with the structure. We can deal with the radon leak. We can bring back the clocktower, and I can't think of anyone else better suited for the job than you."

I stared at him; he had clearly been doing a lot of thinking to have made such a drastic change. "You're asking me to turn down the opportunity of a lifetime to stay in Golden to rebuild an old clocktower," I said.

"I understand," he said, looking away. "Believe me, I get it."

"I'm going to do it, though," I said. "I want to hear the clocktower chime again. Like I said, I've missed home. I'm going to turn down the Chicago offer, so you'd better make sure I've got a job after that committee meeting." I stuck out my hand.

He stood there, staring at it in shock, and his face broke into a massive grin. He shook my hand, then pulled me into an embrace.

We hugged each other for tight, and I tried to ignore how perfectly I fit into his arms.

After a moment we released each other and the two of us walked back together to enjoy some of Aunt Laverne's butterscotch buttons before the rest of the monsters at the parade could snatch them up.

It looked like I was home for the long hall.

Thank you for reading MURDER AT THE CLOCK TOWER I hope you love Hope and Dustin as much as I do.

If you loved fast-paced fun try **A FIRST DATE WITH DEATH**. Some are in it for love... others for the cash...Georgia just wants to stay alive...

And don't miss my **YAPPY HOUR** Series. It's sweet and funny and you'll laugh out loud as Maggie, not quite a dog-lover hunts down a murderer. Will Maggie's investigation kill her budding romance with Officer Brooks?

And if you're looking for something magical, try **A WITCH CALLED WANDA**. Will fledging witch Maeve reverse the curs that has Chuck doomed to live the rest of his day as a female dog...or will someone get away with murder?

And sign up here to keep in touch and find out about new books: **www.dianaorgain.com**

# Also by Diana Orgain

### In the Maternal Instincts Mystery Series

Bundle of Trouble - FREE The only thing tougher than solving a murder... giving birth!

Motherhood is Murder Kate joins a new mom group where mischief and murder run rampant.

Formula for Murder A hit-and-run crash catapults Kate into a mystery at the French Consulate.

Nursing a Grudge Kate's budding PI business is threatened when a new PI poaches her
client.

Pampered to Death Spa day has never been so deadly!

Killer Cravings Can Kate juggle being a PI, pregnant, and those cravings all at the same time?

A Deathly Rattle Who shot rival PI, Vicente Domingo?

Rockabye Murder Dancing can be murder—literally.

Prams & Poison Are there too many skeletons in the Victorian closet Paula's is renovating?

Lethal Lullaby Hush, little baby, don't say a word. Killer's gonna find you in Alcatraz.

Cereal Killer Kate and Vicente Domingo solve a mystery in his old town, Golden,

Double Trouble The only thing harder than solving a murder...giving birth to twins...

### In the Love or Money Mystery Series

A First Date with Death Reality TV meets murder!

A Second Chance at Murder Georgia's new boyfriend disappears in the Pyrenees Mountains.

Third Time's a Crime If only love were as simple as murder...

### In the Roundup Crew Mystery Series

Yappy Hour Things take a ruff turn at the Wine & Bark when Maggie Patterson takes charge

Trigger Yappy Salmonella poisoning strikes at the Wine & Bark.

## In the iWitch Mystery Series
A Witch Called Wanda Can a witch solve a murder mystery?
I Wanda put a spell on you When Wanda is kidnapped, Maeve might need a little magic.
Brewing up Murder A witch, a murder, a dog...no, wait...a man..no...two men, three witches and a cat?

## In the Cooking Up Murder Mystery Series
Murder as Sticky as Jam Mona and Vicki are ready for the grand opening of Jammin' Honey until…their store goes up in smoke…
Murder as Sweet as Honey One messy honeypot…
Murder as Savory as Biscuits Now that he's back from serving his country, all police officer, Leo Lawson wants is to ask out the sweetest jam-maker he's ever known, Mona Reilly.

Get Select Diana Orgain Titles FOR FREE

Building a relationship with my readers is one of the things I enjoy best. I occasionally send out messages about new releases, special offers, discount codes, and other bits of news relating to my various series.

And for a limited time, I'll send you a copy of BUNDLE OF TROUBLE: Book 1 in the MATERNAL INSTINCTS MYSTERY SERIES and lots more exclusive content, all for free.

Join now.

ABOUT THE AUTHOR

Diana Orgain is the bestselling author of the Maternal Instincts Mystery Series, the Love or Money Mystery Series, and the Roundup Crew Mysteries. She is the co-author of NY Times Bestselling Scrapbooking Mystery Series with Laura Childs.  For a complete listing of books, as well as excerpts and contests, and to connect with Diana:
Visit Diana's website at www.dianaorgain.com.
Join Diana reader club and newsletter and get Free book

Copyright © 2021 by Diana Orgain

All rights reserved.

No portion of this book may be reproduced in any form without written permission from the publisher or author, except as permitted by U.S. copyright law.

Manufactured by Amazon.ca
Acheson, AB